HOLLY NATHER BOOK TWO

COHEN'S TALE

SARA DANIELL

Cover, interior book design, and eBook design
by Blue Harvest Creative
www.blueharvestcreative.com

Cover model: Caleb Holleman
Cover model photograph by Mindy Durey Photography

COHEN'S TALE
Copyright © 2014 Sara Daniell

All rights reserved. Except as permitted under the U.S. Copyright Act of 1976, no part of this publication may be reproduced, distributed, or transmitted in any form or by any means, or stored in a database or retrieval system, without prior written permission of the publisher.

This book is a work of fiction. The characters, incidents, and dialogue are drawn from the author's imagination and are not to be construed as real. Any resemblance to actual events or persons, living or dead, is entirely coincidental.

Published by
Opine Press

ISBN-13: 978-0692352373
ISBN-10: 0692352376

Visit the author at:
Facebook:
www.facebook.com/saradaniellauthor
Twitter:
@DaniellSara
Website:
www.saradaniell.com

Purchase other books by Sara Daniell in print, eBook, or audio by scanning the QR code.

ALSO BY SARA DANIELL

HOLLY NATHER SERIES
A Life Unexpected
Daughter of a Monarch
(coming 2015)

THE RIVERBEND SERIES
WITH J.L. HACKETT
Collide
Desolate

To my daughters who remind me to always use my imagination, no matter how old I get.

I was never one to patiently pick up broken fragments
and glue them together again and tell myself
the mended whole was as good as new.

What is broken is broken—and I'd rather remember it
as it was at its best than mend it and
see the broken pieces as long as I lived.

~ Margaret Mitchell

PROLOGUE

AND THEN THERE WAS TUFF…

MOM HAS ME RUNNING ERRANDS FOR HER AGAIN. IT'S NOT that I mind, it's that I wanted to do something else. Something fun. I grip the envelopes tightly in my hand. Mom said if I lost them, I would be in big trouble. Sometimes I wonder why she has me do important things. I'm only eleven.

"Good morning, little man! How is your weekend going?" I smile at the man behind the counter who smells odd—sort of like garlic. Without replying, I hand him the mail. "I will get these sent right away." He turns around, and I respect mom's orders by watching him place them into a large bin. *"Don't take your eyes off them until they are in that bin!"* I hear her words in a tone as if I were already in trouble as the letters drop safely into the bin.

I pick up my pace as I leave the post office. Time for fun. I stop at the local market to use the few dollars I have to buy a chocolate bar. As I'm walking through the woods back home, I hear a rustling sound, followed by laughter in a tree. I look up, crumpling the chocolate wrapper, and place it in my pocket.

"Is someone up there?" I yell. Instead of a reply, I hear more laughter. I finally spot a girl about my age, maybe younger, in a tall tree. My father taught me what is safe to climb and what isn't. And that is *definitely* not a safe tree.

"You should come down from there! It's not safe!" I cup my hand around my mouth and yell.

A girl replies from above. "What do you know? I'm fine! See?!" She is swinging from a branch the size of a toothpick, laughing. I shake my head and begin to walk away when I hear a loud thud. *I knew that was going to happen!*

I run to the girl who is now holding her arm. She has her eyes tightly shut, and her face is sticky from sweat, but not tears. *How is she not crying?* I look down at her bloody arm. I almost get sick when I notice bones are sticking out.

"I can't believe you're not crying! You have to be the toughest girl I know."

Her green eyes glare up at me. "Stop trying to talk to me and go get help, stupid!" I don't say anything else and quickly head toward town.

I run as fast as I can. When I find the nearest adult, I quickly say, "A girl in the woods hurt herself really bad! Can you please help her?!"

The man comes running with me, following my lead. Once we reach her, he quickly scoops her into his arms and hurries back to town. I run after them, and once we reach the healer's house, I sit down in the yard and wait to see how she is. After an hour, the girl walks out of the house with the man who helped her. She has her arm in a sling and a smile on her face.

"Thank you," she says with a smile that goes all the way to her eyes.

"Man, you sure are tough!"

"Ah, it's no biggie…just a broken bone."

"What's your name?" I ask. I know I've seen her around school before, but I think she's younger than me.

"Holly Chophit. I've seen you at school. You and my brother sometimes play together, I think." She's looking around as she speaks. Her expression is hard to read. It's almost as if she's trying to find more trouble to get into.

"What's your brother's name?"

"Harim Chophit. He's my twin." Once she says that, I know exactly who she is. She's the girl who's always by herself at school. Harim told me his sister didn't like spending time with others.

"Well, Tuff, it's nice to meet you."

"Tuff?"

"Yeah, it's what I'm going to call you. After taking a hit like that and not crying, you can't just be called Holly…You need a nickname."

She laughs and swings her head, so her hair goes behind her shoulders. "You're weird. But, I guess it's nice to meet you, too."

PART ONE

I'M IN LOVE WITH MY BEST FRIEND

CHAPTER ONE

THE PAST: WHEN I LET HER GO.

I STOP PAINTING FOR A MOMENT AND COVERTLY LOOK IN her direction. She's reading a book and is so enthralled by the words, that she hasn't moved a muscle for over an hour. I smile inwardly as I take in how beautiful she is. Her dark hair falls perfectly across her cheek bones, blowing slightly in the breeze. It doesn't make sense how a girl can affect me like she does. Just being near her is intoxicating. I hide it well, though. If she knew she gets to me the way she does, it would complicate things. I quickly push my thoughts aside and start painting again before she catches me staring at her.

I've been helping Harim paint the fence around his house for the past week. With it being the last few days of summer, I wouldn't have agreed to this, but his mom begged me, and he *is* one of my best friends. I place my brush down to get a drink, and when I go back to reach for it, it's gone. I wipe the sweat from my forehead and without even turning around, I say, "Tuff...I know it's you."

"Then come get it!" I hear her say through laughter. I turn around with an evil grin and see her running as fast as she can, the brush gripped tightly in her hand.

As I run after her, I yell, "It's really cute that you think you're faster than I am!"

She starts to run faster, but ever-so-gracefully trips over a rock and lands face first on the ground. *It was only a matter of time before she ate dirt.* I quickly sit on top of her so she can't move, and pin her arms to the ground. Smiling, I take the brush from her hand and paint a large white streak across her face.

"You think you are so bad ass," she says, trying to free herself from my death grip.

"One day, you will admit that I am." I get off so she can get up, and she punches me in the arm. I follow her to the pond that's nearby, so she can wash the paint off her face. "Why do you want to wash it off? It covers up the ugly!" My smart-ass remark gets me another punch in the arm. Good thing she's a girl and punches like one.

She rolls her eyes and sighs. "Maybe you should paint your whole body, then."

I laugh, taunting her. "I don't understand why you insist on punching me all the time. Instead of pain, it feels like a flea taking a piss on my arm."

"Ha, ha," she groans from her position at the water's edge. I laugh and sit down to wait while she scrubs the rest of the paint from her cheeks.

"What do you want to do tonight when I get done helping your brother?"

"I was thinking about just staying home tonight. Harim and I haven't really hung out much lately, and he has a new video game he's been dying to show me." I'm not sure how to respond to her. For the past seven years, we've spent practically every night together. "Don't look so shocked. We can hang out with other people, you know."

"I know that. I heard there's a party at the Hole tonight, anyway."

She dries her face with the bottom of her shirt and whips her head around to look at me. "You wouldn't dare go to that party!"

"And why not?!"

"Cohen…" Her hands are placed firmly on her hips, and she is tapping her foot. She's so damn adorable when she's trying to be bossy.

I half grin. "I believe I make my own decisions. Besides, what could it hurt?" I know how Holly feels about parties, *especially* at the Hole.

"Whatever! Do what you want." She starts walking back toward her house.

I catch up with her, pleading. "Don't be mad. I promise I won't get into any trouble."

"I'm not mad. I just don't want you getting drunk. You know what happened last time…"

"I promise I won't get drunk." She puts a fake smile on her face and continues walking. When we get back to her house, Harim is busily painting the fence. He glances my way and then directs his attention back to the fence post again.

"Holly, are you going to let him paint, or play more childish games?". Harim asks laughingly, dipping his paint brush into the bucket of paint.

"He's all yours!" she says, picking her book up off the ground. Holly turns to walk into her house, but not before pausing to give me a *you-better-not-get-drunk* look. I give her an evil grin, and she rolls her eyes while walking into the house.

"I hear you're stealing her to play video games tonight…" Harim doesn't look at me when I speak. He just continues painting.

He dips his paint brush into the bucket again and starts on a new fence post. "You both need to spend some time apart. It's sickening how many hours you two spend together. Plus, I miss my sister."

"You could hang out with Stella." My words cause us both to laugh. Stella is… Well, Stella is just *Stella*.

"What are *your* plans for tonight?" Harim asks, taking a break from painting.

I continue to paint and mumble, "The Hole."

"You're an idiot."

"So I've heard. It's not that big of a deal. Just a bunch of drunk Fae having a good time. Besides, it's your fault since you're stealing Holly for the night."

"You have other friends. You don't have to pick the stupidest thing you possibly could. Wait. What am I saying? I mean, go! Because under-age drinking is a *brilliant* idea!" I laugh at Harim's sarcasm.

"All of my friends will be there, too."

"And your friends have poor judgment! How do you guys get all of this alcohol without getting caught?"

I shrug my shoulders and set the paint brush down. "We have our ways. And stop acting like you've never been to the Hole!" I laugh when he avoids my accusing eyes. "Anyway, I better get home. My dad needed me to do a few things before I went anywhere tonight."

"Okay. I'm thinking about using a bit of magic to paint the rest anyway," he says, placing his paint brush down.

"You sure you want to waste a few months of your life? I can help you tomorrow."

"It's only a few months. It'll be fine." I help Harim gather supplies and clean up the mess.

When we're done putting everything away, I leave to go home… but not before turning to look toward Holly's bedroom window. To my disappointment, I don't see her.

CHAPTER TWO

"FINALLY SHOW UP TO DO SOME WORK FOR YOUR OWN family?" my father says, taking another drink of something strong.

"Cut him some slack, Finn," my mom says while slaving over the stove. "He's always working—if not for you, then for someone else." My mom smiles in my direction and continues cooking.

"Hell, that boy doesn't know what work is. I've—"

I stop my dad before he pisses me off. "Dad, I'm here now. What is it that you wanted me to do today?" My dad takes another drink and then places his cup firmly down on a coaster, causing a loud thud. His scruffy, dirty appearance would have you think he belonged in the mountains, living off the land. It's hard to believe he's high up on the food chain in Gaia.

He clears his throat and takes another drink. "Never mind. You can do it another day. I was going to have you check the gutters on the house. I noticed some hanging the other day. Damn storm." I nod my head and then quickly walk to my room, before he has another chance to make me feel like shit.

I undress from the clothes spattered in paint and throw them on the floor. I take a quick shower and get ready. I haven't been to the Hole in a while. A year to be exact. It's the only thing to do besides sit at my house and rot. And when dad is home, I avoid my house as much as possible. There are parties going on there every weekend, but ever since Jenna disappeared, I haven't gone back. I need to move past that and just go have a good time.

I get to the Hole, which is located in the middle of nowhere in the woods of Gaia. Everyone is around a huge bonfire and already drunk as hell. I make my way over to them, grab a cold drink, and pop the top off with my thumb. I see Tallon leaning against a tree talking.

Too drunk for his own good, he slurs, "Damn it, boy! I thought I may never see you again! Glad you came tonight!" He slaps me hard on the back, causing me to almost drop my drink.

I make eye contact with a girl who hasn't stopped staring at me since I walked over here. I ignore her provocative stare and focus on Tallon. "You know I'm not big on social events."

"You used to be."

I take a drink, and it burns as it slides down my throat. "Fae change."

"What are you doing here tonight, then?" he asks, grabbing another drink.

I shrug my shoulders. "I had nothing else to do."

The girl who keeps staring says, "I know of something you could do…"

I mouth *"no thank you"* and take another long hard drink. She pouts for a minute and then starts hanging on Tallon like he's some sort of god's gift to Fae.

"Where's Harim?" Tallon asks, sitting on a cooler.

I lean against a tree and take another drink. "At home, I guess. Why?"

He shrugs his shoulders and hands me another drink as soon as I finish off the first. "Just figured he would be here."

I cock an eyebrow at Tallon and laugh. "At the Hole? You know he doesn't like this place."

"And neither do you, but *you're* here."

"Like I said earlier, I had nothing better to do."

After too many drinks and too many invitations from girls who mean nothing to me, I decide I better leave. There's a slight problem with that—I am drunk as hell. I stumble around for a while, trying to find my way home. With everything spinning and as dark as it is, getting home isn't easy. I realize I'm closer to Holly's house than my own, so I head that way and unintentionally pass out in her front yard.

"What in the world do you think you're doing?!" I groan and crack an eye open at the sound of Holly's shrill voice.

"Did I fall asleep in your yard?" I ask, rolling onto my back and wiping grass from my face.

"Obviously, genius." She has one of her hands placed firmly on her hip and a cup of water in the other—most likely iced down. Before I can even beg her not to, she dumps the whole glass over the top of my head.

"*What did you do that for!*" I jump to my feet and shake the frigid water from my hair.

"I was *going* to wake you up with it! At least be glad you saw it coming instead!" she says in a sassy tone.

"Damn! I'm up!!!"

"Well, I wasn't going to waste it!"

"You could have drunk it!"

An evil grin forms on her lips. "But, that was *so much* more fun."

I laugh and create a dry shirt. I run my fingers through my cold, wet hair and glare at her evilly.

"Why did you get drunk?" I shrug my shoulders at her question. She isn't the slightest bit satisfied. "Cohen, getting drunk can get you into trouble. Plus, you promised me you wouldn't!"

"I didn't have that much to drink. Lay off, okay?"

"Oh, really? Are you listening to yourself talk right now?! You fell asleep...in my damn yard! What if—"

"Drop it," I say, walking toward her house. I'm hungry and have a headache. Helen always has something cooked, and I'm sure they have some sort of pain reliever.

Holly follows me as I walk into the house. Helen is in the kitchen washing dishes, and as expected—food is ready to be devoured.

"Well, don't you look extra nice this morning," Helen says sarcastically over her shoulder as she takes in my appearance.

"He got drunk last night." I hear Holly mumble a few more unsavory things under her breath. *I really wish she hadn't said that.*

Helen turns the water off and whirls around. "Cohen, if I told your mother—"

"Please don't," I beg. Harrumphing under her breath and giving me a warning glare, Helen drops the subject, thankfully. She rummages through a cabinet and then hands me some pain pills and a glass of water. Tossing my head back, I swallow them both down and return my glass to the counter, nodding appreciatively at Helen.

"I'm not looking forward to going back to school tomorrow. That place is such a bore," Holly says through a mouth full of food. I laugh and shake my head at her. It's so damn cute she doesn't care a thing about manners.

I smile as I think about all her rude mannerisms and the fact that I find them attractive. She has no idea what she does to me. "Yeah, I'm not happy either, but it's life. You'd think that you loved school. You're at the top of your class!"

She rolls her eyes. "Might as well make the best of it."

I shrug my shoulders. "I guess."

"Maybe you'll finally make some friends this year. You need to have friends other than Cohen," Helen adds, sitting down to read the newspaper.

"Holly—make friends? You must be dreaming," I hear her say from behind me. *"Her"* is Stella, but Holly insists I'm not allowed to refer to her by her first name. Holly and *"her"* have never gotten along. Sometimes I forget Stella's even a part of the family.

The girl, whose name I'm not allowed to mention, sits down at the table to eat, and Holly gives me the "look". I know what that means. Time to get up, even if I'm *not* done eating. Just to piss Holly off, I completely ignore her and continue to shovel food into my mouth. She narrows her eyes at me and kicks my leg under the table. I laugh and finally rise to put my empty dishes in the sink.

I follow Holly to her room, and after successfully slamming her door shut, she spins and looks at me, her eyes blazing. "What is her problem?! Ugh, who cares if I don't have tons of friends? Who is she to—You know what? Never mind. It's not even worth wasting my breath over."

Waving her hand dismissively in the air, she takes a deep breath, fighting to regain control over her anger. Looking up, she smiles, and completely changes the subject. "So, what do you want to do today? It's our last day of freedom until next summer."

"We could go to Paradise. We haven't been there in two days." She looks thoughtful and then starts rummaging through her drawers. She pulls out a bathing suit, and I try hard not to replay images of her wearing it. I fail. Plopping down on her bed, I smile to myself while she goes in her bathroom to change.

"Ready?" she asks when she appears. I nod my head and open her bedroom door, letting her out first.

CHAPTER THREE

HOLLY TAKES OFF RUNNING INTO THE CRASHING WAVES. I take off my shirt and turn my shorts into swim trunks. I race toward her and jump into the water. After swimming for a while, we sit on the shore, close enough for the waves to barely touch our feet.

"Cohen... What am I going to do when you graduate this year? You're the only one who gets me at school. I don't want to follow Harim around...that would be embarrassing for his sister to be everywhere he is."

"Why don't you stay out of the library, put down your books, and try to meet other Fae?" She looks at me with a *yeah right* look and laughs. Holly definitely isn't a social butterfly—far from it.

"Socializing isn't *my thing*. I'll be fine. Books are way more interesting anyway."

"You won't know until you try."

She laughs. "I *have* tried. And I failed. Let's talk about something else, please."

"What do you want to talk about?" I ask, laying back on the sand, placing my hands behind my head.

"What are your plans after graduation?"

"Work. Most likely carpentry. I really like building things."

She smiles. "I figured that. Your dad isn't going to make you work for him?"

"New subject, please." I hate talking about my father.

She rolls her eyes. "Okay...I'm going to ask you a question, and you have to answer it honestly. Then you get to ask me one."

"I'm always honest," I lie. I haven't been honest about my feelings for her.

"Favorite color."

I laugh and sit up. "You already know that."

"No, I know what it was two years ago. It could have changed."

"Well it hasn't. It's still gray."

"How can you like gray? That's such a boring color!"

I gently nudge her shoulder and say, "Hey, it's my turn to ask you a question." She laughs and pretends to zip her mouth shut. "Who's your favorite Fae?"

I didn't expect her to blush at that question. It's adorable. "Stella." She bursts out laughing.

I laugh with her. "You have to be honest, remember?"

"Right. Well, I must have lost my mind saying this out loud, but...it's you. You're my favorite Fae."

"So, you're finally admitting that I'm bad ass?"

She rolls her eyes. "No. I'm admitting that you're my favorite Fae to be around. That has nothing to do with how *bad ass* you are. You're such a nerd."

I smile. "Your favorite nerd."

She laughs and then becomes serious. "Hey, Cohen..."

I sit up and look at her. "What?"

"Do you ever wonder what kind of dad you would have made?"

I close my eyes and take a deep breath. "Holly, don't." She ignores my request.

"Seriously, Cohen. What if she didn't run off?" Her eyes are intense and determined.

I look out at the water and try my hardest to keep my temper in check. "She *did* run off. There's nothing else to think about. It is what it is. Now please...just drop it!"

Her expression shows her concern, but I don't need anyone being burdened about this. "You don't talk about it enough, Cohen. I think you should."

I clench my fists and begin to shake. "It's been a year, Holly! It doesn't help me to talk about it!"

Casting her eyes down, she whispers, "Sorry…I just think about it a lot."

"And I try not to." I sigh, gazing out over the water.

CHAPTER FOUR

IT'S THE MORNING OF THE FIRST DAY OF MY SENIOR YEAR. Nothing feels very special about it. Just another year of boring lectures. I run my hands through my hair to mess it up just right, and then head out the door after giving mom a hug.

When I get to school, I see Holly leaning against the wall, reading a book. As usual. On my way over to her, a few of my friends stop me and start talking.

"We're at the top of the food chain, boys!" Tallon boasts, throwing his arm around my shoulders. I shrug him off and laugh.

"Cohen, why haven't we seen you all summer? You still obsessed with the Chophits?" Drake taunts in a smart ass tone.

"I'm not obsessed. They're just cooler than all of *you*." I duck when he takes a playful swipe at my head.

The bell rings, and I look over my schedule to make sure I'm headed to the right class, when I run into Holly in the hall. "Watch where you're going, bookworm."

She looks up and smiles. "Have fun today. See you at lunch." She continues walking to her class as she reads her book—not paying any attention to where she's going. It will be a miracle if she makes it to class without face-planting in the hall.

Once I get to my first class, I sit down in an empty chair at the back of the class and goof off with my friends. The teacher silences us and starts our math lesson. I definitely didn't miss the sounds of pencils on paper or the yawns and sighs of the bored students. I only pretend to listen to the lecture, counting the minutes as they tick slowly by.

Finally, the bell rings. I gather up my things and head to study hall. When I walk in the room, I spot Holly sitting in a desk in the back. I quickly make my way back there and sit down in the desk in front of her.

"Isn't it great we have a class together?" Holly says with a huge smile on her face.

"Yep. Maybe this year won't be too bad after all." I smile and turn around in my desk. I notice Daniel watching Holly, and the way he's eyeing her hungrily makes the hairs on the back of my neck stand up.

I want to put up a huge sign that says MINE. I somehow restrain myself from doing so, but still manage to shoot him an evil glare. He doesn't even waver. This just seems to make him that much more eager to go after her. He gets up and casually walks over to her desk and leans against the wall. I recline back in my desk and cross my arms over my chest, glaring at him with a disgusted look on my face.

I scoff at him as he begins to talk. "Looking good this year, Holly."

"Hey, Daniel," Holly says, sticking her nose further into her book. I chuckle under my breath at her attempt to ignore him.

"Maybe we could hang out this weekend?" Damn. Daniel is an idiot.

"Maybe," she says, smiling at him. I straighten up in my chair and look at her like she's lost her damn mind. She shoots me an icy stare and then smiles back at him.

After they finish their sickening small talk, I sink lower into my chair. *Great. The one class I have with her, and now I have to share it with a guy she may be interested in.*

"What's your problem?!" she hisses.

"He's no good for you," I growl back, discretely peeking over my shoulder to ensure the teacher isn't watching.

She looks past me at Daniel and then whispers, "I don't think that's for you to decide." I shrug my shoulders at her stupidity and turn around in my desk. It's possible that I'm being an asshole...No, not likely. I can judge the intentions of others well, and his definitely aren't good.

Holly doesn't talk to me the rest of day. She ignores me in the halls and after school, heads straight home. Being the persistent ass that I am, I go straight to her house.

"She's pretty pissed at you." Harim is sitting on the front steps, as if he were waiting for me. "You need to go home. Let her calm down some."

I laugh coldly. "Pissed at *me*?! Daniel was the one trying to talk to her! Don't tell me you would approve?"

"She has to make her own mistakes, Cohen. We've protected her for too long. Which hasn't even been a hard task. She doesn't date or talk to anyone besides us. Let her make some decisions on her own, okay?" Harim is being unreasonable. Daniel is trouble, and he knows it.

I run my hands through my hair and feel my temper rising. "You can't be serious?!"

Standing up to hover inches from my face, he says through clenched teeth, "Leave it alone. She isn't *yours*. Maybe you should tell her how you feel...*then* you can act like an ass about it. But, until that day, leave her dating life the hell alone!" I laugh and push Harim out of the way, storming up to Holly's room.

Maybe I *am* being a territorial ass. But I don't care. I know I should tell Holly how I feel, but I don't know how. I open her door to find her lying on her bed, looking at a picture of her dad.

"What makes you think you can just barge into my room like that?!" She bolts upright and places the picture firmly on her nightstand, hard enough to cause a thud.

I shove my hands in my pockets as a smart-ass smile tugs at the corners of my mouth. "I always *just barge in like that*."

"Well, it's not okay when you do something like you did today! You are such an ass, Cohen!"

I shrug my shoulders. "Sorry."

She rolls her eyes and takes a deep breath. Letting it out, she relents, "Why did you act like that when Daniel talked to me?" Her big green eyes are pleading with me to tell her the truth. But—I can't tell her the complete truth.

"Because, I *know* Daniel. You don't. He's trouble, Tuff."

"Maybe. But it's still possible that he's changed over the summer." She has her arms crossed over her chest and a few strands of hair are falling in front of her face. I almost can't refrain from going over to her—moving the hair from her face—and kissing her breathless. My pulse quickens at the thought of sharing such an intimate moment with her. I push those thoughts from my head and glare at her. I want to shake her and tell her how naïve she's being. Instead, I shrug my shoulders and say the worst possible thing I could say. "Go out with him, then."

"I am. But, thanks for the permission. *Not!*" Now she's smiling, and I can tell she's excited. I work up a fake smile and laugh. I'm not worried. I'll be saying, "*I told you so*" after all this is said and done.

CHAPTER FIVE

I WAIT IMPATIENTLY WITH HARIM ON THE FRONT STEPS OF their house. Holly is way past curfew and is still out with *Daniel*. "What do you think is taking her so long?"

"Maybe she's just having a good time." I smack Harim in the back of the head. "What?! Maybe she is," he says, rubbing the back of his head.

I take a deep breath and let it out. I jump to my feet when I finally see Holly walking up. I groan when I see that Daniel's still with her. Holly rolls her beautiful, but angry eyes when she sees me and Harim waiting up for her.

"Don't you have a house?" Daniel asks. I notice he's holding her hand, which almost knocks the wind out of me. I don't reply. Instead, I nudge him hard enough with my shoulder to cause him to stumble a little as I walk past him. As I head toward my house through the dark woods, I curse under my breath.

When I get home, I go straight to my room. I close my bedroom door and turn on some music. I strip down to my boxers and flop onto the bed. I *am* being a total ass. It's *my* fault I haven't told Holly how I feel. I'm afraid she won't feel the same way, or be willing to start up a relationship with me. Then things would be weird between us. My biggest fear is us drifting apart. I look down at my Fae ring, hoping for the day it might glow the same color as hers. I am so damn pathetic.

I begin to drift off to sleep, when I hear a loud thud at my window. I see Holly unsuccessfully trying to get in, so I hastily get up to help her through.

Holly climbs in and puts her index finger firmly on my chest. "Cohen, you're going to have to accept the fact that I'm going to date! I know we're best friends and spend all our time together, but you have to let me hang out with others sometimes!" Holly being in my room makes my mind go places I really shouldn't be thinking about right now.

Taking my mind off *other* things, I push her finger away and apologize. "I know. I was an ass. I'm sorry."

She sits down on my bed and sighs. "He was a jerk anyway." I want to say *I told you so*, but I don't.

I try really hard not to laugh. "Do you want to talk about it?"

"No, not really." She lies back on my bed, and I lie down next to her. She contradicted herself, because right now, she is talking nonstop about how uninterested she is in him. This makes me happy. Ecstatic even.

After she's done venting, I say, "Sorry you had a bad time. Although, that's what you get for bailing on your kick ass best friend." She punches me in the arm and laughs.

"I guess I'm just going to have to marry you. We spend all of our time together anyway!" My breath is knocked from me for the second time tonight, and it takes me a minute to accept that she's just joking. My mind wants desperately to accept the words as truth.

Recovering quickly, I reply, "Marry *you*? No thanks." I laugh when she punches me again.

"Want to go toilet paper Mr. Neely's house? I have all the supplies right outside your window." I find myself focusing on the movement of her lips instead of the words coming out of her mouth. "Cohen? Did you hear me? Want to go?"

I get my thoughts together and laugh. "You are *such* a bad influence on me."

She rolls over and rests her head on her hand. She raises her eyebrows and grins mischievously. "Is that a yes?"

I take a deep breath and let it out, pretending to ponder the idea just to piss her off. "I guess." She jumps ecstatically to her feet when I finally agree. After I get dressed, we sneak out my window, and not only does she have loads and loads of toilet paper, but she also has alcohol. I raise my eyebrows at her.

"What?! I've never been drunk. Thought I'd try it. But I want to be with you when I do it. You won't let me make a fool out of myself."

I shake my head. "I can't let you get drunk, Tuff."

"Fine, I'll do it without you, then." That's an even worse idea.

"Fine! But when I say you've had enough, you have to stop." She rolls her eyes in consent, grabs a hand full of supplies, and starts walking.

Holly is on her sixth drink and can barely throw the roll without falling. I catch her before she hits the ground. "That's enough. No more. And I think we've added more than enough toilet paper to Mr. Neely's trees. Time to get your drunk ass home."

Through slurred words, she mumbles, "I can't go home like this." She's right. *Damn it.*

"Want to stay the night at Paradise?" She nods her head and stumbles. Chuckling to myself, I easily sweep her up into my arms and carry her the rest of the way.

Upon arriving, I create a tent with my abilities, along with some blankets and pillows. I gently lay Holly down. She couldn't help but pass out while I carried her here. I lay awake watching her in her drunken slumber, trying to convince myself to come clean with her about my feelings. However, by the time I actually fall asleep, I'm already talking myself *out* of telling her the truth.

CHAPTER SIX

"I AM NEVER DOING THAT AGAIN!" HOLLY YELLS BETWEEN wretches, as I hold her hair back while she pukes. "Why did you let me do that?"

"Umm, I clearly remember telling you it was a bad idea."

She groans as she continues to vomit. When she is finally done, she runs to the water and jumps in, clothes and all. She walks back out, dripping wet, holding her head in her hands.

"Headache?" I ask knowingly. She nods her head almost imperceptibly and sits down gingerly beside me.

"I bet Mr. Neely is *pissed* this morning," she says, using her abilities to dry her clothes.

"Probably. I bet our parents are even more pissed we aren't at home getting ready for school."

"Ah, they expect it. They know we run off together."

"Yes. But it isn't summer anymore. I'm sure they'll be pissed that we're missing school."

Holly shrugs her shoulders and lies back in the sand. She looks up at me while I stare down at her, waiting for her to say something. But she doesn't. I want to ask what she's thinking about, but I'm enjoying sitting in silence with her green eyes staring into mine.

"Why don't you date anyone?" Out of all the questions she could ask, she asks me this?

"I haven't found any girl worth my time yet."

"You spend every waking minute with me. How could you possibly meet other girls? Maybe we should stop hanging out so much." That is the worst plan in the whole entire universe. I start to object, but stop when I see Harim walking through the trees.

"Why aren't you guys at school?" Harim asks while observing Holly's appearance. Her hair is a mess and she has dark circles under her eyes.

Holly places her hands on her aching head. "Stayed out too late and fell asleep here."

Harim laughs. "I saw Mr. Neely's house. You two aren't responsible for that, are you?" Holly makes brief eye contact with me and laughs.

"Maybe," she says, as an evil grin spreads across her face. "Maybe not."

"Right, because it's not at all obvious that you two did it." Harim rolls his eyes as he points to the left where toilet paper rolls lay scattered all across the sand. I frown in confusion as I think back to last night...I have no idea how they got here; we left all the supplies behind when I carried Holly here in her drunken stupor. I furrow my eyebrows in concentration, thinking harder. *Nothing.* Not a single hint as to how everything mysteriously showed up in Paradise. I throw a bewildered expression at him and shrug, unsettled. I guess I'll just have to chalk it up as unexplainable or I'll go crazy trying to figure it out. Harim sits down next to me and cocks an eyebrow, looking at me suspiciously. "Just how much trouble did you two get into last night?"

I glance at Holly before I answer. I'm not sure if she wants to tell her brother about her little drunken episode or not. Her face remains emotionless. "Your sister thought it would be a good idea to get drunk. I didn't drink anything so I could play babysitter."

"That's dumb," he says, glaring at his sister. Holly picks up a pile of sand and throws it at him. I laugh and stand up to stretch.

"Don't worry. I won't ever do it again. I feel horrible this morning." Holly stands up and begins walking toward the trees to leave. "You guys coming? We better let our parents know we missed school before the school calls to tell them."

I walk in the opposite direction to go to my house. When I walk in the door, I see my mom sitting at the table sipping coffee.

"Where were you last night?" she asks, anger brewing in her green eyes as she sets her cup down.

"With Tuff. We fell asleep at Paradise."

She looks pissed. She slowly takes another sip from her coffee while peering up at me over the rim of the glass. "Her mother came to see me this morning."

I lean against the wall and run my hands through my hair. I slide my hands into my pockets and look down at my feet. "And what did she say?"

"She said Mr. Neely's house was decorated in a lovely shade of white. When will you two grow up? You're a senior in high school, Cohen! You have to start getting serious about life! And you and that girl spend way too much time together. It isn't healthy."

I laugh at my mom and ask, "And why is it not healthy?"

Her expression becomes more serious, if that's even possible. "It just isn't."

Changing the subject, I say, "I'm going to take a shower and sleep for a while. I didn't get any sleep last night."

As I start to walk off, my mom says sternly, "No more missing school. It's only your second day after summer break, and you skipped. If your father finds out, you are going to be in a *lot* of trouble."

"Is he going to find out?" She shakes her head reluctantly, and I let out a sigh of relief. She's probably being too easy on me, but I appreciate it all the same.

CHAPTER SEVEN

AFTER A NAP, I HEAD BACK TO PARADISE. I NEED TO TELL Holly *exactly* how I feel. It's not fair to keep it from her. When I get there, I see her sitting against a tree, reading a book. As she looks up at me, I notice she has a black eye. I pick up my pace to reach her faster.

"What happened to you?!"

She laughs coldly. "My sister and I got into a fight. It's no big deal. I'm fine. Stella, on the other hand…"

I kneel down beside her, moving her hair out of her face to look closer at her eye. "Over what?!"

She turns her head away from me. "Honestly? I don't even remember. One word led to another and then I punched her in the face. Then she punched me back…" She shrugs it off like it's no big deal and starts reading her book again.

I snatch the book from her hands. "You two have to stop this! She's your *sister*!"

Grabbing the book back, she glares at me. "Whose side are you on?"

"Neither. You're both in the wrong."

"Well, Mr. Genius, when you figure out all the messed up dynamics of our relationship, then tell me. Until then, I'm going to continue to dislike her…a lot." She's so cute when she's angry, which distracts the hell out of me.

I sit down next to her and lean against the tree. "Do you ever *try* to get along with her?"

She shakes her head. "That would be pointless. She hated me first. I know it's because so much responsibility was thrown on her after my dad died. But that's something I can't help. I just don't get it and honestly…" She shrugs her shoulders and looks at me, "I don't really care."

I know she cares. I know it hurts her. Tuff has always been bad about hiding her true feelings. Every once in a while, she'll open up and tell me her deepest, darkest thoughts and feelings, but sometimes, she just locks her thoughts up so tight that nothing could get inside that stubborn head of hers.

Changing the subject, I ask, "Did you get in trouble for missing school today?"

"Nope. Did you?"

I shake my head no. "How's the headache?"

She points to her black eye. "Worse."

I came here semi-prepared to tell her how I feel about her, but now I've chickened out. Staring at the girl who gives my simple life meaning makes the words I long to say mute. It's as if they're ready on my tongue, but when I go anywhere near her, they back the hell up and take off running back to my brain to hide safely.

She looks thoughtful for a moment and then says, "I miss my dad. I know I was only three when he died, but I remember him. Tall and smelled like an old dusty book…I guess that's why my sister and I got in that fight. Harim and I were talking, and somehow my dad came up. Stella, being the horrible sister she is, laughed at us both. She said there was no way we could possibly remember him—that we were too young. I told her she had no right telling Harim and I what we do and don't remember! Those are *my* damn memories! I know my brain didn't just make them up!" I didn't expect her to open up like this. I thought we were off the subject of the fight. But, I let her vent. "Cohen, I know you and your dad don't have a relationship, so you can't understand, but it really hurts!"

"I do understand. I understand because I long to have a relationship with my father. And my own child. Me and you sort of go through the same pain in the 'father' category."

She sets her book beside her and rests her head on her knees. "Your situation is worse, Cohen. I would rather have the short time I did with my dad, than him be alive and non-existent to me. Or... well, never mind."

I shrug my shoulders and look out over the water. "It is what it is..."

"Do you ever wonder if you have a daughter or a son?" Holly knows I don't talk about this.

"Holly..."

"You're the one who brought it up! You have to talk about it, Cohen! I know you think about it! It must kill you inside!"

I look down at the sand and take a deep breath. I have a really bad temper, and I try really hard not to lose it with Holly. "What happened with Jenna that night...shouldn't have happened? I was drunk, and so was she. She got scared and ran off to God only knows where. Damn..." I feel tears burning my eyes and my voice is getting shaky. "Let's talk about something else."

In barely a whisper, she squeaks out, "I don't want to talk about something else. You haven't fought for your child, Cohen!"

I lose it. She has no right to talk to me about this. I stand up and start to walk away. Holly runs after me, pulling the back of my shirt. I whirl on her, inches from her face. I jab my index finger into her collar bone and glare down at her. "Don't you *dare* begin to tell me what I have or haven't done! You don't know that I've gone out nights when I should be sleeping, searching everywhere for them! I've gone to her house to see if her parents have heard from her or know where she is! No one knows anything about her! They don't even know she was pregnant with my child! This is so damn complicated; you couldn't even begin to understand!"

She swallows hard and gently pushes my finger away. "Did you love her?"

"No! Shit, Holly! We have been through this already!"

"I'm sorry I upset you." She looks down at her feet.

I run my hands through my hair and sigh. "I need to go."

She looks up at me with sad eyes. "You need to go, or I made you mad and that's why you're leaving?"

I place my hands in my pockets and look away from her. "Both."

"See you at school tomorrow?" I nod and watch her walk through the tall grass before I leave to go home.

As I walk home, I think about Jenna and the baby. He or she would be a year old now. It kills me that she ran away. We didn't love each other. If we did, she probably wouldn't have run off. Maybe if I lied to her and told her I did, she wouldn't have left. Who the hell knows…What I do know is that I was drunk, and so was she. We were at a party and things happened. I never would have imagined that all of this could have happened from making one mistake that night. It makes me sick to know that my child will never know his or her father. I hate Jenna for leaving. But what Holly doesn't understand, is that there is only so much I can do.

CHAPTER EIGHT

"COHEN!" I HEAR HOLLY'S HIGH PITCHED SCREAM DOWN the hall.

"Calm down, Tuff! What is it?!" She is jumping up and down, causing my classmates to stare. Not that I care, but she is causing a scene.

Her eyes are wide with excitement. "I got called to the principal's office during first period, and I was terrified I was in trouble for missing school, but guess what!"

"What?"

"They told me that if I keep up what I'm doing, I'll get to graduate at the top of my class!"

I nudge her softly in the shoulder and say, "I told you being smart would pay off!"

"I can't wait to tell Harim!"

I see Harim walking toward the cafeteria and point at him. "There he is." Holly takes off running, yelling his name. I shake my head and laugh.

I walk straight to the table in the cafeteria where we always sit. A small round one, big enough for me, Holly and Harim. Sometimes Tallon hangs out with us, but usually he just sits with my other friends I never talk to.

Harim places his food down on the table and beams proudly. "Isn't it awesome Holly is doing so well in school?"

"Kick ass for sure," I agree, propping my feet up in an empty chair.

"Are you not eating?" Harim asks, observing the empty spot in front of me at the table.

"Nope. I forgot to grab lunch from home and what they're serving today doesn't appeal to me." I shudder at the thought of *whatever-that-is* getting anywhere near my mouth. "I can't believe you're eating that shit." Harim shrugs his shoulders and continues to eat.

I notice Holly isn't anywhere in the cafeteria, and I start to get worried. She was *just* behind Harim in line to get lunch. "Hey, where is your sister?"

He looks around and says, "That's strange. Maybe…Never mind, she wouldn't be talking to anyone."

"I'll go look for her." A bad feeling washes over me, and I instinctively pick up my pace. I push past others as I try to find her. I run my hands through my hair in desperation as I look around, and then I finally see her—backed into a corner by Daniel. He pulls his hand back and slaps her hard across the face. An instant of sheer terror flashes across Holly's face as she recoils from him, holding her cheek, her eyes wide in shock and anger. Whatever sense of self-control or composure I had shatter into a million pieces in that moment. I'm on top of him in less than a second, my fists raining down on Daniel's face, over and over, the torrent fueled by the fire of my fury. Holly is screaming at me to stop, but I can barely hear her through the blinding rage behind my eyes. The sounds of students yelling are muffled by my anger, but are growing loud enough to realize that I have an audience. But I don't care. All I can concentrate on is my fists pummeling his face, the blur of red a slick mess under my murderous hands. I am just about to use my abilities to finish him off, when I feel forceful hands grab me from behind and tear me away from the motionless figure beneath me. I'm breathing heavily, sweat pouring from every inch of my body, my hands still shaking violently in an unbound urge to seek revenge. I look down at the unconscious bloody mess that is Daniel, and know without a shadow of doubt in my mind—he deserved it.

Everything appears to be in a haze as I make my way to the office. I am instructed to sit on the bench outside the principal's office. I see healers running down the hall in Daniel's direction and wonder if I really hurt him that badly. I lost any self-control I had. I close my eyes and run my hands over my face. All I can hear is the loud thud of my heartbeat. I feel someone sit down next to me, and I pry an eye open.

"Are you okay?" Holly asks in a hushed tone.

"The question is—are *you* okay?" I reply in the same hushed tone.

"You almost killed him, Cohen."

I replay the image of him slapping her, and the look on Holly's face after. If it weren't for her sitting next to me now, I would go after him again. "He slapped you."

"I was fine. I can handle myself. Now, who knows what is going to happen to you!"

"I don't care what happens to me. Why did he do that to you?!"

"He was mad because I told him I wasn't interested in another date. He said something that pissed me off, so I smarted off to him. He said that no girl would ever speak to him like that, and he was far more superior than any female Fae." I knew he was an ass, but I never would have guessed he'd do something like that. I put my arm around Holly and pull her into a hug.

"He won't mess with you anymore, I can assure you," I say, kissing the top of her head. Why the hell did I just kiss her on the head?!

She looks up at me with suspicious eyes and says, "You just—" She looks at me, confusion written all over her face, and thankfully, abruptly changes the subject. "How can you be sure he'll leave me alone if you get suspended? You know that's what they're going to do to you!"

"I just know he won't." I get up when the principal calls my name. Holly gives me a distraught look as I walk into the office.

"Mr. Aberdeen, what exactly possessed you to cause such harm to your fellow Fae?" the principal asks as his forehead wrinkles with concern.

I look down at the dried blood on my knuckles and smile perniciously. "Sir, you're married, right?"

"Yes. But what does that have to do with your dangerous behavior?"

"If someone caused harm to your wife, what would you do?"

"Cohen Aberdeen, please make your point—and fast."

"I watched as that fellow Fae slapped Holly Chophit in the face." Images of his hand going across her face echo in my mind, causing fury to build again like water bursting through a dam.

"Were there witnesses?"

"While I was kicking his ass, yes. I'm not sure if anyone saw him slap her besides me. I'm sure Holly will tell you everything." I realize I just said a word that would be considered disrespectful in the presence of an adult in authority, but I'm already in trouble. So, oh well.

"I will speak with Ms. Chophit later. In the meantime, I have to suspend you for your actions."

"How long?" I ask.

"Three weeks. I will notify your parents as well. You may go get your things and tell your teachers you will need your assignments mailed to you."

I stand from my chair and nod my head. I hurry out of the office to the bathroom to wash Daniel's blood from my hands. I go get my things and give my teachers the principal's instructions.

CHAPTER NINE

I HAVE AVOIDED MY PARENTS TO THE BEST OF MY ABILITY for the past week. When they found out what I did at school, they didn't hesitate to insist I couldn't be around Holly anymore. They said I cared for her too much and almost took someone's life because of it. I couldn't use the marriage analogy with my parents, because they don't know what love is. They had an arranged marriage.

I sneak out of my room for the first time in a week to go to Paradise. Holly has probably been wondering where I've been. When I finally make it through the woods, I see Harim, but not Holly.

"You were hoping to see my sister, right?"

"No. I was eagerly seeking your presence." What kind of preposterous question was that? *Of course*, I was hoping to see her.

Harim laughs. "She's at home. Your father called my mother and said you were not to see Holly anymore."

His words don't seem to register in my brain. "He did *what*?!"

"You heard me. He said your friendship with her wasn't normal. Holly has been extremely distraught, and has come here every night looking for you. When you didn't show, she figured you listened to your father." I don't say another word; instead, I return home to speak to my ass of a dad.

I forcefully kick the front door in and push my dad out of his lazy chair. His drink sloshes all over the walls and he quickly jumps to his feet.

"Cohen!" he shouts, his voice engulfed in anger.

"What right do you think you have calling Holly's Mother?"

"I am your father!" he says.

"You haven't been a father since the day I was born! *You care more about your drink than you do anything else*! Why start interfering now!"

My dad doesn't say another word. He walks calmly to the kitchen, pours himself another drink, picks up his chair and sits down. Anger doesn't begin to describe what is coursing through my body at this moment. I want to demand that he give me answers, but he is too much of a damned coward to do that. I storm down the hall to my room and slam the door shut. I pick up the phone to call Holly—hoping she answers.

"Hello?" There's the voice I wanted to hear.

"Hey, Tuff."

"You shouldn't be calling me…"

"Well I am, aren't I?"

I hear her sigh, and then she says, "They suspended Daniel, too."

"Good."

"Do you think you and me are too close? I mean…we do spend all of our time together. Maybe it's time we start hanging out with different people."

"Shut up."

"I'm serious, Cohen."

"I am, too." We sit in silence, and all I can hear is her slow breathing.

"Are you there?" she asks in barely a whisper.

"Yes, I'm here."

"I think maybe we should just take a break from each other."

"I don't like that idea."

"See you when you get back to school."

"Tuff…" She doesn't reply. Instead, she hangs up.

I listen to the silence before putting the phone down. I get up and start pacing around my room. I don't know how to handle not seeing or talking to her on a daily basis. But maybe she's right. Maybe we *are* too close…

CHAPTER
TEN

THE WEEKS SPENT AT HOME WERE DREADFUL AND PASSED by slowly. I'm actually happy to be going back to school today. I'm not sure how I feel about seeing Holly. I went to Paradise hoping she would show, but she never did. A lot can change in a few weeks.

When I get to school, I see Holly in her normal spot, leaning against the brick wall of the school. I don't know if it's okay to go talk to her or not, so I stand with my friends, waiting for the bell to ring.

"Daniel is going to seek your death after that stunt you pulled," Tallon says. I don't reply. The mindless conversation about my lack of self-control drones on as I ignore every bit of it.

The bell rings and successfully makes me feel ill. I don't want to go in there and have Holly ignore me. Normally, she would have already said something to me. I need to stop obsessing and just walk my paranoid ass up to her and talk first.

I see her at her locker, stealing a few more moments of being lost in the pages of her book before the second bell rings. I hurry over to her and lean against the neighboring locker.

"What are you reading?"

She smiles without looking at me and replies, "I'm not sure what it's called."

"Did you not read the title?"

"Nope." She's still smiling, but I want her to make eye contact with me. I need to see she's okay.

"And why not?"

"Because. I wanted to read the book first and then read the title." She closes the book backwards so she doesn't see the front, and places it in her backpack.

"You are so weird."

She looks at me. Her eyes are full of curiosity. She's looking at me differently. I know we've spent weeks apart without a single word, but something is…different.

"I've missed you." The words she just spoke make my heart act in a way I thought it forgot.

A smile tugs at my lips. "Me too, Tuff. Paradise tonight?"

She laughs. "Poker? It *has* been a while since I've kicked your ass." We both look up when the second bell rings. We're late. *Damn it.*

After school, I run home and grab the cards and poker chips. I rush to Paradise, and there's Holly, waiting for me.

I smile and tease, "I'm surprised you showed up."

"Why's that?" she asks, sitting down on a blanket she brought from home.

"You don't like losing."

"Oh, come on now. You know me *much* better than that. I don't fear losing because I always win." She starts dealing the cards and smiles at me.

"You always win? Now you're lying." I laugh and go first.

After spending a lengthy amount of time getting my ass whooped, I finally fold. I usually win. I didn't even cut her any slack. She seriously kicked my ass today, and she's a little too happy about it.

As she cleans up the cards, she asks, "What did you do all that time you were suspended?" I wonder what her reaction would be if I answered her question like this,

Thought about you. Longed for you. Forgot how to breathe at times thinking you may never speak to me again. That I was scared as hell you would enjoy our time apart and find new friends.

Instead, I keep my previous thoughts to myself and say, "I did work for my dad."

"That sounds horrible. Working for your dad would be hell. Your dad's a jerk." I don't reply; I don't like talking about him.

"When Daniel came back from suspension, did he give you any trouble?" I ask, changing the subject away from my dad.

She shakes her head no. "I still don't think it's fair that he only got a week. He was the cause of it."

"I almost killed him. I'm lucky they didn't kick me out of school and throw me in jail."

She looks thoughtful and smiles. "I don't think I ever thanked you. It's nice to know I have someone in my life that cares so much about me." She has no idea how much I care.

I smile. "That's what best friends are for, right?"

"Yeah, I would do the same if someone tried to hurt you, too, I guess."

I laugh. "Good to know."

PART TWO
LETTING HER GO

CHAPTER ELEVEN

TWO YEARS HAVE PASSED, AND I STILL HAVEN'T TOLD HOLly how I feel about her. My feelings have grown even stronger. And I'm not sure I'm capable of hiding them any longer.

Holly graduated a year after me, and at the top of her class. I skipped out on college and decided to work instead. I do odds-and-ends jobs for others, but mainly construction work. Sometimes I cheat and use my abilities, but I like living, so I'm usually worn out by the end of the day doing it the hard way.

My mom and Holly's mom found out Mr. Neely, the man we picked on for years, was sick and in the process of healing. They both decided it was a good idea for us to apologize by bringing him a meal.

So, that brings me to where I am now... waiting for Holly at her house. She's in college and doesn't get out of class until this afternoon.

"Are you *really* going to tell her?" Harim asks, laughing doubtfully at me.

"Yes. I've kept it from her way too long."

"Today? On the way to Mr. Neely's?" Harim's face is full of disbelief.

"Yes!" I almost shout.

Harim leans back on his hands and smiles. "You know my sister is unpredictable. She may kill you." I laugh because I know he's telling the truth.

"She might." I look up and see her walking toward us. My palms are instantly sweaty, so I discreetly wipe them on my jeans.

"Let's get this over with," she says with a grimace, peeking into the basket and eyeing some of the containers inside. She told me she didn't mind apologizing to Mr. Neely, but thought bringing him food seemed a little excessive.

On our way there, I don't say much. I'm trying to figure out where to start. This may not be the best time to tell her, but if I don't do it now, I probably never will. I need to do it while I still feel confident about it.

"Hey...Holly?"

She looks up at me, arms wrapped tightly around the basket of food, and breathes, "Hmm?"

"What do you think about us? Our friendship? What exactly is this between us?" My heart is racing, and I'm anxiously searching her expression for an answer.

She stops walking and looks down at the ground. "What do you mean, Cohen?"

"I mean—" I'm suddenly cut off by unfamiliar voices behind us. I put a hand on her shoulder and whisper, "Hey, did you hear that?"

Holly pushes past me and looks through the trees. In a hushed tone, she says under her breath, "No one comes down this road. Who do you think it is?"

"Hello, Ms. Chophit. How coincidental it is running into you here today. I remember meeting your father down this very road many years ago." Holly looks at me when she hears the voice speak her name. I shake my head and nudge her to convince her to keep walking.

"Who are you?" I grab Holly's arm before she can go seek out the voice further.

Three men appear before us, and I immediately know they're trouble. They aren't Fae, nor are they from Gaia. "Holly, let's go," I rasp through clenched teeth.

She pulls her arm from my grip and says, "Versipellis? From Terre?"

"Smart girl. Just like your father...Although *he* showed a lot more fear in his eyes right before we killed him. Are you not afraid, child?"

Holly drops everything in her arms, and I watch as fury rolls off of her in waves. It feels like everything starts moving in slow motion just as she lunges toward them. She has lost her damn mind! There are too many of them; she won't win this fight. I immediately start pulling magic from the magic of the Versipellis. Holly is doing the same, so I start to build my strength off of her magic as well.

Holly looks at me, her eyes pleading with me to do something. What she doesn't realize is that I'm doing everything I can—it's just not working. One of the Versipellis hones in on Holly, not at all fazed by the magic she and I are throwing in his direction. Raising his hand in the air, he knocks her effortlessly to the ground. The other two Versipellis close in on me, but my own safety is forgotten while I watch in horror as Holly struggles to get up. Following my gaze, they smile wickedly as they turn their attention to her.

I hurl magic, packed with as much brute force as I can muster, toward the Versipellis who are now tossing Holly through the air like a rag doll. All the magic I'm throwing at them still doesn't seem to affect them at all, and then suddenly, Holly's body is lying lifeless and drenched in blood on the ground. My heart clenches in anguish, and my eyes burn with a fierce hatred as I stare down the Versipellis who did this to her. My gut reaction is to stand and fight, make them pay for what they have done, but the sight of Holly lying broken and bleeding rips at my soul. Throwing one last murderous glare at their smug and victorious expressions, I teleport us both to the nearest healer's house.

"Boy, what is wrong with you? Bursting through our doors uninvited!"

"Sir, she's *dying*! Please help her!" I beg in frenzied desperation, tears pouring from my eyes.

They don't ask any more questions and quickly take Holly from my arms, laying her flat on the ground. I fall to my knees beside her and grasp her hand, pleading with her to come back to me. The healers are doing everything they can, but nothing seems to be working.

"Go get her mother," one of the healer's demands in a rush. I don't hesitate. I let go of her hand and quickly teleport to her house.

Harim is outside and when he sees me he shouts, "COHEN?!" His eyes land on my shirt and hands, both covered in blood, and the color drains from his face.

Straining to catch my breath, I yell through labored gasps, "It's Holly! Get your mother!"

Harim sprints into the house, returning almost instantly with his mother, Stella, and Helen. "*Where?*" Harim yells, his voice panicked.

The five of us teleport to the healer's house, appearing right outside the door. I follow Harim and the others as they enter the house, but one of the healers stops me. "Are you and the girl blood-related?"

"No, sir."

"I'm sorry. Family members only." He turns to walk into the house, but I grab him by the shirt, yanking him back to me.

"*I. Am. Going. In.*" I growl through clenched teeth.

He calmly pulls my hand from his shirt, retreats into the house, and slams the door in my face. I pound my fists on the door, demanding to be let in, but eventually give up when I realize I'm being an ass. They have a job to do, and Holly needs her family right now.

Trying to distract myself from what may be a long wait ahead of me, I use my abilities to change my clothes and clean Holly's blood off of me. By the time I'm done, I'm completely drained of emotion and energy. I lay my head against the side of the house and close my eyes, every fiber of my body willing Holly to make it through this.

I open my eyes and lurch toward Harim when he appears in the doorway. "How—" I barely get the word out when Harim shakes his head, his eyes glued to the ground, refusing to look at me. I find the wall for support as Harim falls to his knees and sobs so loudly I'm sure all of Gaia can hear him. *This can't be happening. Holly can't be gone.*

My legs feel like they're about to give out, and I slump to the ground, trying desperately to wrap my mind around this. I rake my hands over my face, and tears I didn't know I had left come flooding out of me.

I hear the door open, followed by quiet footsteps. I look up through a wall of tears to see Holly's mother completely shattered. "Harim. Cohen. She's breathing now."

Harim and I jump to our feet. "She's alive?! But, they declared her dead?!" Harim chokes in hopeful disbelief.

"She's in a coma. The healers aren't sure if she's going to make it, but we can only hope for the—" Her voice breaks and she starts to crumple to the ground, but Harim catches her as she sobs heavily in his arms. Stella is leaning against a tree—her face completely devoid of emotion. I rush into the house and past the healers, ignoring their yells for me to leave. I dash into the room where Holly lies on a bed, still drenched in blood.

"Can't someone clean her up?" I yell, focusing my abilities on removing the blood from her hair and clothes.

I feel a hand on my shoulder and turn to look into Harim's somber eyes. "Cohen, the healers are resting. They made a huge sacrifice by doing what they did to get Holly back. They could have let her die the first time they declared her dead, but they kept trying. They took many years off of their own lives to try to save hers."

"Well, then what would a few more hurt by getting her cleaned up?" My tone is cold and harsh. There is no excuse for allowing her to lay drenched in blood.

"We're bringing her home. You should go home and get some rest. I will notify—"

"I'm not leaving her, Harim."

CHAPTER TWELVE

I HELP HARIM BRING HOLLY BACK TO HER ROOM AND GET her settled in bed. I collapse into a chair in the corner and close my eyes wearily. The same question keeps echoing over and over again in my mind. Why wasn't I strong enough to stop the Versipellis? Fae are supposed to be stronger, and there were two of us. As anger and guilt begins to build once again, I stand to my feet and restlessly start pacing around Holly's room.

"Cohen, what's wrong?" Harim asks, concern evident in his voice.

"This is all my fault. It's my fault this happened. I tried Harim, I swear I did. I…I don't know what went wrong." I'm not sure if he even understood anything I just said through my hysterical sobbing. Harim advances on me, a stern expression on his face as he places a firm hand on my shoulder.

"You can't blame yourself for this. I'm not sure what happened, but I *do* know how you feel about her, and I know you would have gladly died in her place to protect her."

Stella walks into the room and interrupts, "Cohen, your mother is on the phone. She's worried about you."

"I don't want to talk right now. Tell her I'll be home soon." Stella nods her head and leaves the room. Harim also leaves, and I'm not sure how I feel about being in here alone with her.

I look at Holly, who appears to be only sleeping, and then have to quickly look away. *Come on Tuff, wake up.* I sit down next to her in the bed and gently pick up her hand and place it in mine. I lean my head against the headboard and close my eyes. I start to drift off to sleep, but quickly shake myself awake. I watch her chest move slowly up and down as I force my eyes to stay open. I rub her hand gently with my thumb and kiss her on the top of her head.

The door cracks open and Harim tacitly peeks his head in. In a low voice, he whispers, "You're going to have to go home and get some rest."

"I can rest here. I'll just lay awake at home." Harim nods his head and quietly closes the door. I drift off to sleep.

I wake up and realize I have my arms wrapped tightly around Holly. She hasn't moved a muscle. I try to suppress my rising anger, but it only builds stronger. I try to concentrate on breathing evenly so I don't completely lose it.

"Tuff," I beg. "Please. *Please* wake up. I am so sorry I didn't do more." Tears start flooding from my eyes.

"Staying here isn't going to help you feel better." I startle when I hear Holly's mother speak. I didn't even realize she was in the room.

I stand up and pull back the curtains on the window to look outside. I see the white fence and remember the day when Tuff took my damn paintbrush. I chuckle and turn to look at her mother.

"Can I have a moment alone with my daughter?"

"Of course." I turn to leave the room, but her mother stops me before I can exit.

"I know how much you love her. You should know she loves you, too. She told me yesterday morning." A tear falls from her red, swollen eyes.

I don't reply. Instead, I leave the room and quietly close the door. I lean against the wall in the hallway as I meditate on the words that just left Ms. Chophit's mouth. I feel shaky, as if my legs may give out any second. I slide down the wall to the floor. *She loves me?!* I'm not sure whether to be happy or mad. Anger wins. I quickly stand to my feet and sprint down the hallway. I race down the stairs and through the front door. I keep running as fast as I can to Paradise and begin pulling so much magic, it must be taking thousands of years off my life. But, I don't give a damn. The only thing keeping me from taking my own life is the possibility that Holly could still wake up.

"Stop! You are going to kill yourself!" I hear Harim yell from behind me.

"*Why didn't our rings glow?*"

Harim looks down at his feet and then his gaze meets mine. "Cohen…She took her ring off before she admitted it to herself. She wanted to tell you without the rings telling you first."

I fall to my knees and sit down on the sand, running my hands through my hair. "She has to wake up. Damn it, she *has* to."

"I know. And she will." Harim says, handing me Holly's ring. I twirl it around in my fingers and then make a tight fist around it.

"I'm going to find them. They will pay for what they've done."

"That's not a good idea. You don't need to get yourself killed. The Peace Keepers of Gaia are searching for them and have notified Terre's leader." I peer curiously at Harim as he speaks. How is it that he can remain so calm? I feel like I'm dying inside.

I don't respond. I stand up and solemnly place Holly's ring in my pocket. I walk back to her house and make my way back up to her room. The healers are tending to her, moving her legs and arms in an effort to keep her blood circulating. I sit in a chair to watch. My stomach churns violently at the sudden realization that Holly may never wake up.

CHAPTER THIRTEEN

I JUMP WHEN I HEAR STELLA ENTER HOLLY'S ROOM. I didn't realize I had fallen asleep. "Helen cooked breakfast. Would you like for me to keep watch while you go eat?" she asks, sitting on the bed next to her sister.

I cut my eyes at her. "Why do you hate her so much?" Her eyes fly open wide in surprise at my candid question.

She straightens out the blankets on the bed as she responds in a curt tone. "I think you should go eat and not burden yourself with things that don't concern you."

"Answer me! She has done nothing to you! All these years, she has longed for your approval. She would never have admitted it, but I know that's what she wanted. Now you may never have the chance at a real relationship with your own sister!"

With fury filling her eyes and venom dripping from each word, she seethes through gritted teeth, "Go. Eat."

"Not until you explain," I demand.

She stands up and tries to compose herself, but loses the battle. Her fists clench, and her eyes blaze as they bore into mine. "She stole my childhood from me! She and Harim both! I had to grow up and be a damn *parent* because my own mother couldn't even get out of bed. She was catatonic for *months* after my father died, and so messed up for so many years afterward, that I didn't have time to be a sister. We never had the kind of childhood we both deserved, and I don't think

I'll ever get over it! I didn't even have a chance to mourn the death of my own father. Instead, I had to be the only parent we had left!" She breaks down in hard, racking sobs, and I'm not sure what possesses me to do it, but I wrap Stella in my arms.

Stella accepts my embrace and sobs uncontrollably into my chest. "Cohen… She loves you so much. When she would come home after hanging out with you, she would be all giddy like girls are when they're in love. I overheard her talking to my mother yesterday morning, and she admitted to being in love with you. She said she wanted to tell you, but was too scared she'd mess up your friendship if you didn't feel the same way. I'm sorry I've been so hateful. I didn't know how to be a sister to her or Harim after being their mother-figure for so many years. Helen was a great help, but wasn't involved as much as I wished she'd have been. Mother is better now, but…I just can't explain what it was like around here after my father was killed."

I gently ease out of the hug and look down at Stella, seeing her in a totally different light. I understand her now. I watch as she moves her hair out of her face and I realize, for the first time, just how much she and Holly look alike. I close my eyes and try to imagine Holly…my Tuff…*awake*. I open my eyes and realize Stella has left the room.

I lean down close to Holly's cheek and listen to her breathe. "Holly," I whisper through trickling tears. "Please come back to me." I kiss her softly on her cheek and then head downstairs for breakfast.

As I eat, I find myself growing increasingly angry when I realize everyone is going on about their day as if everything is perfectly normal. I know that's the right thing to do, but I can't pretend as if my reason for breathing isn't lying unconscious upstairs, struggling for her damn life.

Interrupting my rancorous thoughts, I hear Helen's voice directed my way. "Your mother is very concerned about you," she says as she scans through the newspaper.

"I'm not leaving until Holly wakes up," I grind out in finality, forcing another bite of food into my mouth. Unable to listen to another word of their unburdened chatter, I tune out the voices around me until they're just a dull drone in the back of my mind. As soon as my plate is empty, I retreat back up to Holly's room. I close my eyes and take a deep breath before opening the door. I pray for a miracle.

As I place my hand on the doorknob, I hear quiet sobs coming from within and slowly ease the door open just a crack. I realize Holly's mom is the one crying. She has her head laid across Holly's chest, begging and pleading for her to wake up. I hastily close it again and wipe the sudden tears away from my own eyes.

Damn it, why didn't I do more? Was there anything else I could have done?! And WHY didn't our magic work against them?! Remembering back to the Versipellis and their gloating faces, unadulterated fury engulfs me like a flash wildfire, threatening to consume every inch of me. I struggle in vain to refrain from destroying everything within reach, but before I even realize what I'm doing, my fists are hurling into the wall.

"*Cohen*!" I barely hear Harim's harsh reprimand through the haze of my anger, but continue throwing punches into the wall, blood dripping from my knuckles with every blow.

"Stop!" I hear Holly's mother scream. I take a few deep breaths while I try to gather control of myself. The adrenaline is starting to wane and my balance falters. I succumb to the exhaustion that is slowly taking over my body, and allow myself to slump to the floor. I bury my face in my hands, now covered in blood, and a fresh deluge of tears start anew, pouring from my eyes in gut-wrenching anguish.

I feel her soft, comforting hand on my shoulder and become aware of her kneeling beside me. What the hell is wrong with me? *I should be comforting her.* "I'm sorry."

"Cohen, you have nothing to apologize for," her mother assures me in quiet conviction. She's so calm, so in control...and I can't help but wonder how she does it?

"You don't understand. I have every reason to apologize! It's *my* fault your daughter is fighting for her life right now. I should have done more! It should have been me!"

"Cohen, don't say that. I know how deeply you feel for my daughter. And I know you did everything you could do. Please, don't blame yourself." Holly's mother pats my shoulder soothingly and I nod my head numbly. As she stands to her feet, my eyes drift from the damaged wall to my bleeding hands.

"I will fix the wall." I stand up, trying to remain calm, and she laughs at me.

"Don't worry with that, dear. You need to go get your hands taken care of, and then spend some time with my daughter. She needs you." Using my Fae abilities, I quickly mend the damage done and she laughs at me again. "Thank you, Cohen. Now go get yourself cleaned up. You can use Holly's shower if you'd like."

"Thank you. Are you sure you don't mind me staying here?"

"If Holly were awake, she wouldn't want you to leave. It wouldn't do her or you any good if you went home. I talked to your mother, and she is sending some clothes and things over for you." A foreign feeling crosses face as a smile tugs at my lips, the first since Holly's attack.

"Thank you," I breathe in relief. She smiles warmly, a soft expression in her eyes, and pats me on my back before she walks down the hall.

I open the door to Holly's room and go to the bathroom to take a quick shower. My hands burn as the soap and water run over them, causing me to clench my jaw tight. After my shower, I use my abilities to make myself some clean clothes and get dressed.

When I exit the bathroom, I find Harim covering Holly with a blanket. "Hey," I say, throwing my towel in the dirty laundry basket.

"Are you okay?" he asks.

I laugh acidly. "Am I okay...*am I okay*?!" I grab a nearby chair and throw it against the wall, watching it smash to pieces. "I will *never* be okay until *she* is okay!"

"Cohen..." Harim looks at his sister and then back at me.

My voice softens somehow, but my hands are still trembling in rage. My jaw is clenched tight, barely allowing words to escape my lips. "Look, I know you're hurting, too. You're just handling this situation a whole lot better than I am. I don't know how to act like all of this is okay."

Harim doesn't reply, instead deciding to leave the room. I pick up the pieces to the chair I broke, and then go lay next to Holly on her bed. I pull her hair back from her ear and whisper softly, "I am so sorry I let this happen to you."

CHAPTER FOURTEEN

HOLLY HAS BEEN IN A COMA FOR ALMOST THREE MONTHS. Yesterday was her birthday. I came home last night when they decided to celebrate it like she was awake and well, and could actually enjoy it. I wasn't in the mood for dinner and a cake, knowing the birthday girl was still in her never-ending slumber, completely oblivious to the rest of us. I admit I've entered a state of depression, but with Holly in a coma, I just can't find anything to be happy about. I reach for my pants when I hear an unexpected knock at the door. I quickly slip them on and open my bedroom door.

"Stella? Is everything ok? What are you doing here?" Stella is standing at my bedroom door, struggling to catch her breath. "Stella! What is it? Don't tell m—"

"Cohen." I immediately start to run, but feel Stella's hand on my arm pulling me back. "Wait!" she yells.

"Is she gone?!" I ask, tears beginning to flood my eyes. I'm not ready to hear this, but I brace myself for the news anyway.

I close my eyes as she speaks. "Cohen, Holly's awake."

A blast of air leaves my lungs and my eyes snap open as the tears finally spill over. "Awake?!"

"Yes. But, she doesn't remember any of us. She's lost her memory. Maybe you should go see her; if there's anyone she'll remember, it will probably be you." My brain isn't sure how to process this. I've spent every day of the last twelve years with her. How could she not remember me? *Impossible.* In stunned disbelief, I push past Stella and race to Holly's house.

I run straight up to her room and stop at her door. Taking a deep breath, I try to mentally prepare for what I'm going to see in there, and knock softly. Harim comes to the door and whispers conspiratorially in a low voice, "She's scared out of her mind. She thinks I'm lying to her about who and where she is; she thinks she lived in another world. Be patient with her, Cohen." I search his face and nod my head, pushing past him slowly. I close the door behind me and stare at Holly...at my Tuff...sitting up in the bed, looking around suspiciously.

I try to say something, but nothing that comes out of my mouth could be considered intelligible speech. I'm stuttering like a fool, trying to figure out where to begin, and wholly unable to pry my eyes away from my beautiful girl, awake at last.

Holly looks scared as hell. She peers nervously at me and asks impatiently, "Are you just going to stare at me all day?"

I laugh at myself as I try to speak, but still fumble over every word. "Sorry, I...I just don't know what to say."

In a rude tone, she says, "How about you start by telling me why we are best friends."

I have to remind myself that she doesn't remember. Every muscle in my body yearns to go wrap my arms around her in a tight embrace, just to make sure she's real. An errant thought crosses my mind. Maybe she's just playing a joke on all of us? That's totally something Holly would do. My gaze rakes over her skeptically, but I quickly realize there's no way she's joking about this. She wouldn't be able to keep a straight face with me, let alone the blank, expectant expression currently residing on her humorless face. Suddenly, it's as if a dam gives way that's been holding back all my anger and now it's bursting forth, running free in reckless abandon throughout my body.

"*Why don't you remember?*" I yell in frustration. She flinches away from me, tears promptly spilling down her cheeks, and I feel like a total ass.

"Because I don't! Do you honestly think this is easy for me?" She bolts up from the bed and starts hurling things around the room while crying and screaming. I rush to her side and wrap my arms around her, whispering my apologies and soothing words as I try to calm her. *Once again, this is all my fault.* She's fighting me like a wayward child, trying to remove herself from my grasp, but I only tighten my arms around her, my own tears brimming over.

In barely a whisper and crying, I say in a soothing tone, "Shhh, Tuff. Calm down. It's going to be okay. I am sorry I overreacted."

She pulls herself from my grip and looks at me like I've lost my mind. She leans against a wall, trying to gain her composure, and asks sheepishly, "What is that you just called me?"

A smile tugs at the corners of my mouth. "Tuff. It's your nickname. I've been calling you that for years."

I spend the next half hour explaining how her nickname came to be. I point out the scar on her elbow and reach out to touch it, but immediately withdraw my hand when I feel a slight shock pass between us where our skin made contact. I stare at her in wide-eyed disbelief. My blood is boiling, and the feelings I already feel for this girl are multiplying by the second. *This cannot be happening. Not now! Not like this!* I force myself to pull away from Holly. I suppress the urge to rush back to her and touch her again, just to recreate that *spark* again. Instead, I stare at my hand and then back up into the sad eyes of the girl who owns my heart and soul. She is scared and begging for an explanation, but I don't know what to say to her. How can I possibly explain my feelings for her now, when she doesn't even remember me or our amazing friendship? It would only scare her more. I decide to just play it off like I don't understand it either.

Holly narrows her eyes at me, but doesn't question me further about what happened when we touched; instead she asks me about her accident. I almost don't tell her. I don't want to relive that, not for a single second…But she deserves to know, and I should be the one to tell her.

After answering her questions the best I can, I decide I'd better leave and let her get some rest. Not only that, but I need some time to myself to think and process all this. She doesn't remember me or anyone else. And, why would touching her *now* be any different than it was before?

As I'm leaving Holly's room, I see Harim. "Hey, can I talk to you?"

"Sure. How did it go in there?"

"Before or *after* I touched her arm and our abilities accepted one another?" Upon hearing this, Harim's eyes enlarge to the size of saucers.

"No *way*." I nod my head and don't know whether to laugh or cry. Just my luck—things would finally start coming together with Holly when she didn't even know my name. Perfect. "Did you tell her what happened?"

My eyes snap to the ground, and I swallow hard, taking a deep breath. I finally look up into Harim's face and nod.

His eyes widen almost imperceptibly, but I hear his sharp intake of breath. Before he can even ask, I offer him the truth. "I had to, man. She asked, and she's lost three months of her life because of it. She deserved to know, and I needed to be the one to tell her. After everything that's happened to her, I couldn't lie to her about this. I owe her that much."

Harim sighs, and then dips his head, accepting my answer. "You're right. She needed to know. How did she take it?"

I rake my fingers through my hair, heaving out some pent-up frustration. "She was confused at first, not understanding why anyone would want to hurt her. But overall, I think she took it well. She didn't really say much."

"So, what now?" Harim asks, leaning against the wall.

"I help her to remember. I refuse to lose her again." I walk past Harim and continue down the hall.

CHAPTER FIFTEEN

I TOLD HARIM TO HAVE HOLLY MEET ME AT PARADISE. BUT only if she wanted to. I would have invited her myself, but she seems to trust Harim more than anyone else right now. I'm waiting anxiously for her to get here, but it's looking like she may not come. I start to head down the path that leads to her house, but stop when I hear Holly walking and mumbling to herself. I lean against a tree and fold my arms across my chest.

When I see her, I start walking toward her and half smile. "Hey Tuff, thought you may stand me up."

Holly looks at me funny as a playful grin appears. "I thought about it, but when Harim said 'Paradise,' I decided to come." I nudge her gently on the shoulder for her snide remark. She pushes me back, causing me to almost run into a tree. She's laughing, and I almost feel like crying, I've missed the sound of it so much.

As we continue to walk, I look at her sympathetically. "How are you doing? I mean with not remembering anything?" I ask.

She scratches the top of her head and looks confused. "I don't know…This is all so confusing. All I can think about is Luke from my dream.

"Luke?"

"Yeah, my husb—" She laughs at herself and stops talking. She shakes her head and looks up at me. "You know what…It doesn't matter; it was just a dream." I can tell her mind is trailing off somewhere else, and her thoughts are obviously disturbing.

I stop walking when I realize she almost said *husband*. I fold my arms over my chest and stare at her. "Were you about to say husband?" Shocked does not begin to describe how I feel right now.

She scrunches her nose and snickers. "Yeah…Weird right?"

"You're too young to be married, and I didn't approve of him. So, you are right; that had to have been a dream." I smile when she cocks an eyebrow at me.

"Oh—so I will need your approval?"

What she doesn't remember, is that we made an oath when we were thirteen. "Yup, that has been our agreement for a long time."

She furrows her eyebrows and looks down at her feet. "You know…" She stops talking for a moment and then looks back up at me, "The fact that I don't remember anything is kind of unfair. You could tell me practically anything, and I have to agree to it and believe without question that what you tell me is the truth."

I laugh. "Good thing I'm trustworthy." I give her an evil grin and continuing walking. "Or am I?"

We reach the tall grass, and Holly stops walking, eyeing me skeptically. I laugh and pull back the thick patch of grass stretching far above us. I gesture with my hand for her to go first and hold the grass back as she hesitantly walks through.

Arriving on the other side, her facial expression at this moment is priceless; she is in complete awe. It seems a bit silly to me, since we've spent practically every day here together for the last twelve years, but I have to keep reminding myself—she doesn't remember.

"Oh wow!" she exclaims as she peers out at the crashing waves. I smile, watching her make her way onto the sand and take everything in.

I remove my shirt before running headlong into the crashing waves. When I surface from the water, I see Holly sitting down. I yell over the sound of the waves to ask why she isn't coming in, but I can't hear her response. I'm guessing it's probably because she doesn't have on a swim suit, although that wouldn't have stopped her before. Normally, she'd just use her abilities to create one or say "to hell with it" and jump in with her clothes on. Again, I have to mentally shake myself. *She doesn't remember Cohen...She doesn't remember.*

I want to get out, but she seems to be lost in thought, and I don't want to interrupt whatever's going through her mind. So I swim for a while.

When it doesn't seem like Holly will be resurfacing from her reverie anytime soon, I finally get out and use my abilities to dry myself as I walk toward her. She's looking at me curiously, but I don't question it.

"How did you do that?" she asks.

"Do what? Swim? Oh, that is easy."

She punches me in the arm. "No, stupid! How did you dry yourself off so quickly?"

Laughing, I say, "I know what you meant; I'm just teasing you. That's one of the cool things our Fae abilities allow us to do." I sit down next to her and nudge her gently in the side with my elbow. "What were you thinking about while I was swimming? I could tell you were in deep thought." I wasn't going to ask, but I can't help it...I want to know.

I grin as I watch her cheeks turn red. "Just about my dream."

"Tell me about it." I lie back in the sand and fold my arms behind my head.

"Seriously?" She sounds surprised that I asked.

"You bet. I want to know what was going on in that crazy head of yours while you were missing out on spending time with your kick-ass best friend. It sounds like you were one busy girl."

"You have no idea." She begins to tell me everything about her dream. There are times I want to interrupt, but I resist, listening attentively to every word.

When she's done talking, I look at her, studying her face intently. "That is a *very* detailed and long dream. But I guess it would be long; you were asleep for three months."

"Yeah, I guess." She sighs. "Cohen?"

"Yeah?" I ask, looking at her.

She looks thoughtful for a moment and stares at the sand. "Would you think I'm crazy if I said I didn't want the healers to make me forget?" She looks embarrassed for even asking.

I study her for a minute and then shrug my shoulders. "No. If it makes you happy to remember, then there is no reason anyone should make you forget."

"Yeah…It's just…I'm scared I will never get over Luke, even if he is some made-up person. He was so real to me."

I really dislike this Luke. My expression turns grim for just an instant, but I hurriedly force my lips back into a smile. "Unless…You fall in love with someone else. That would help you get over him." I can't believe I just said that. I almost don't look at her, worried I may have offended her.

"Maybe," she says, shrugging her shoulders.

The sun is starting to set, and I know I'll have to bring Holly home soon. I watch as she looks down at her scar, fixating on it. She runs her index finger across it slowly, and I see her eyes peek over at me. She quickly averts her gaze back to her arm and continues to run her finger across it. I'm about to get angry. Not with her; she can't help this. But fate has seriously pissed me off. Why the hell did this happen to her? To us?! We were so damn close to being together! Taking a deep breath to calm myself before I completely lose it, I decide we both better go home.

"You should probably head home. It's starting to get dark," I say, standing up and brushing the sand off my clothes.

She pulls herself out of her inner thoughts and up to a standing position. "Yeah, the healers are coming. What should I tell them?"

I continue to suppress my almost-temper-tantrum and shrug. "Tell them what you feel is best for *you*. They won't do anything if you don't allow it."

She looks at me with a strange expression. I can tell she knows something has changed with me all of a sudden. She sighs, resigned. "Okay. Well, I guess I better go. I had a good time. Meet you here tomorrow?"

"You have to train tomorrow. How about I come watch you train so I can laugh at you?" I smirk, trying to lighten the mood. It seriously sucks that she doesn't remember me.

"You better watch out. Once I gain control of my Fae abilities, I may be able to take you down."

"Yeah right! If you had any recollection of me, you wouldn't be saying that. I'm pretty bad ass."

"We'll see about that. My nickname is Tuff after all."

I shake my head and laugh. "Only because you fell out of a tree and didn't cry."

She rolls her eyes and says, "See you tomorrow then?"

"Wouldn't miss getting to see your ass kicked for anything."

I watch as she makes her way through the tall grass. I offered to walk her home, but she refused. She's trying to be independent, and I understand that. Sort of. I make my way through the grass and head home. All I can hope for is that the healers will help her remember. If they can't, then I'll do my best to help get her memories back…

CHAPTER SIXTEEN

WAITING TO FIND OUT IF HOLLY REMEMBERS IS TORTURE, and I decide that I can't wait until morning. Jumping out of bed, I sneak out of the house and head straight to her house. I knock at the door and wait.

Harim opens the door and smiles. "Hey. She's asleep. Want me to—" I interrupt what he's about to say and push past him. I hurry up to her room and quietly open and close to door. I lean against the wall and look at her. She is sound asleep. I almost wake her up, but decide against it. She needs her rest.

My hands begin to tremble at the thought that the healers might have been unsuccessful. *Please remember me.* I start to pace the perimeter of her room, and I think about what I'll do if she *does* remember. I found out she *does* love me. If she remembers, do I say something about it? Or do I just wait for her to tell me? Do I give it time? Will she even remember that she forgot all of us for a while?

And then…what if she doesn't remember? How long do I try to help her remember? What if she decides that she hates me? I start to leave the room, thinking I'd rather Harim tell me if she remembers or not. That way I'm more prepared to face her with either fate. As I start to walk toward the door, I hear her sit up in bed. I stop walking and turn to look at her. I hold my breath as she opens her mouth to speak.

"I don't remember anything."

Anger consumes me, and I swing the door open. Harim, her mother, and Stella practically fall through the door frame. I shake my head at them and push past them all, storming out the front door. I almost go home, but decide to sit on the front steps instead. I need to talk to her. I need to tell her everything. Even if she isn't ready to hear it. I can't hold this in any longer. Who gives a damn about the timing being right?!

Several minutes pass as I take in the solitude of the evening, wondering how to finally tell Holly the news I've kept secret for so many years. Breaking through the stillness of the night, the front door swings open, and Holly comes barreling out of the house, tripping over me in the darkness. I quickly stand and help her up. She looks at me with wide eyes and says accusingly, "I thought you left! What are you doing here at this time of the night, sitting on my steps?"

I run my hands nervously through my hair. I watch as her expression changes and then softens. I sigh and say gently, "I never left. I've been sitting here since I left your room."

"Why?!"

I shrug my shoulders. "I just couldn't leave. Damn it, Holly, it's not fair! Why did this happen to you? Why wasn't I strong enough to do something to stop them?" I am on the verge of tears and am shocked when Holly wraps her arms around me.

"Cohen, it's okay! Bad things happen to good people all the time. It never makes sense why things happen, but all we can do now is move forward and go on with life. Please don't blame yourself."

I take her arms and peel them off of me and instead, wrap my arms around her. She lays her head against my chest, and for just a moment, I almost forget that she doesn't remember me. "You're the one that needs the hug, not me. I just get so angry about what happened. I should have done more."

Holly looks up at me and smiles. "Even though I don't remember the past, I can honestly say you are the best friend I have ever had. I know you did everything you could. Please don't blame yourself."

I almost lose every bit of self-control I have. I brush loose strands of hair out of her eyes and pull her tighter against me. She quickly pulls herself from my embrace, and I can see her hands shaking. She sits down on the steps, and I hesitate before sitting down beside her. I almost kissed her. *Damn it, Cohen.*

I try to lighten the mood by nudging her a bit with my shoulder. She smiles and pushes me harder, causing me to fall off the step altogether. We both convulse into laughter, and before long, we're having trouble breathing. After I'm finally able to catch my breath, I sit down beside her again. I pat my shoulder, inviting her to rest her head there. She hesitates.

I laugh. "There is no rule that says best friends of the opposite gender can't lay their heads on each other's shoulders." I scoot closer and pat my shoulder again.

"I guess not." She smiles and lays her head on my shoulder. I put my arm tightly around her.

"Hey, Tuff?"

"Yeah?"

"Thanks."

She picks her head up and looks at me with a confused expression. "Thanks? For what?"

"For waking up."

"That is a silly thing to thank someone for. I mean, I didn't really have control over it." I reply by shrugging my shoulders and smiling. She lays her head back on my shoulder, and before I know it, she's sound asleep.

CHAPTER SEVENTEEN

AFTER I HELP MY DAD WITH A FEW THINGS, I HEAD TO HOL- ly's to watch her train. Plus, I need to talk to Harim. When I get there, Harim is outside working on the landscaping. When he sees me, he stands up and walks toward me. I stop where I'm at and wait. I run my hands through my hair and take a deep breath.

"You look upset," he says, rubbing dirt off his hands onto his pants.

"I just wish she'd remember. It's killing me. Especially now that I know how she truly felt about me. I'm so damn stupid for waiting all these years to tell her. Why did I wait, Harim?!"

Harim frowns and shakes his head. "I'm sorry that you have to live with that regret. But, you have to move on from that. You—" Harim stops talking abruptly when he sees Holly walking toward us.

"So what is the deal with the cryptic look on your faces?" she asks with a huge grin on her face.

"Nothing," we both say in unison.

She places her hands on her hips expectantly and taps her foot. "Explain."

"Cohen, you got this one, buddy?" Harim asks with a half-smile.

"If I said I was not ready to talk about it, would you let me explain later?"

She rolls her eyes. "Okay, but we *will* be talking about it later."

I am thankful she has decided to drop the subject, for now at least. We all walk to their backyard, where Tib is supposed to be meeting them.

As he and Holly are training, the subject about her Fae ring comes up. I get a bit uncomfortable and start squirming in my seat. I hope they forget about it and move on. After Tib gets done explaining what it is to her, Harim offers to go get it for her. I give him a worried glance, and he returns it with a re-assuring smile. After Harim walks off, I hear Holly ask Tib about the day of her accident.

"If our kind are sooo powerful, then why couldn't Cohen and I fight those Versipellis that tried to kill me?" Holly looks at me after asking that, and I immediately look away.

Tib takes a deep breath and lets it out. "I am not sure what happened that day, but there should have been no reason you and Cohen couldn't have killed all three of them. It was most likely your nerves."

She looks down. "Oh…" She turns to look at me again, and I look up to meet her eyes. I somehow manage to move my mouth into a half smile. She smiles back and turns to look at Tib.

"So…about this channeling magic thing. The other day, Cohen touched my arm—" Her words stop abruptly when I jump to my feet.

Quickly trying to change the subject, I turn to Tib. "Tib, shouldn't you do less talking and some *actual* training?" My eyes are pleading with him to say yes.

Tib looks confused, but then agrees. "I guess we should." He stands up and holds his hand out to help Holly to her feet.

My attention is diverted when I notice Harim walking toward Holly with her Fae ring. When he places it in her hand, she is shocked by the bright light that shoots out from it. We all laugh at her surprised expression. After she gets over her initial shock at how the ring responded to her touch, she asks which finger to put it on. I clear my throat and tell her to place it on her left ring finger. She twirls it around in her fingers, studying the ring, and I smile when she notices the inscription I had engraved on it.

"Tuff?"

I look at her and smile. "I had it engraved when you were in a coma." She smiles and looks back down at her ring.

I watch as she hesitates before putting it on. As she slides it onto her finger, I inhale sharply when Harim grabs my arm and we both see it glowing orange. Harim and I immediately look down at mine, which is also glowing orange. I don't know what else to do, so I run, headed straight for Paradise.

As soon as I get there, I start pacing around the beach. I can't stand still. This is so damn crazy! How is this even possible?! She doesn't remember me, yet her ring is glowing the same color as mine! I drag my hands through my hair and look down at my wrist. I curse under my breath. There it is. There is the damn mark. I feel Holly standing next to me and deliberately ignore her as I try to process all this and figure out how I'm going to explain it all to her.

I turn to her and point to her left wrist. She glances down at her wrist like she's checking her watch, and immediately looks up at me like I'm crazy. I reach out and flip her wrist over so her palm is facing up. She looks down and gasps. Her shocked eyes find mine, and I can see a million questions blooming there. And then I raise my arm to reveal the same mark emblazoned on my own wrist.

"Holly, do you know what this means?" She shakes her head no. I take her hand and lead her to a shady part of the beach. We sit down together, but I don't let go of her hand. How am I going to explain this to her without making her hate me?

"Cohen, what is going on?" she asks, her eyes full of worry.

This is it. I have to tell her. "Holly, I am in love with you." She quickly pulls her hand from mine. I watch as tears fill her eyes, and her face pales. I take her hand again and grip tighter so she can't let go. "I wanted to tell you, but then you got hurt and—"

She interrupts me and tears fill her eyes. "Cohen, stop."

I grip her hand tighter and yell. "No! You have to hear this! I don't give a damn if you don't feel the same, but you deserve to know how I feel!"

"Stop!" she screams.

I ignore her pleas and continue. Lifting my free hand to her face, I turn her chin so she has to look at me. "Holly, I adore you. I always have. I just never knew how to tell you. I was going to tell you the day we met up with the Versipellis. That mark," I say while turning her wrist up to reveal it, "would not be there if you didn't feel the same."

She snatches her wrist from my hand and jumps to her feet. She turns the opposite direction from me and runs her shaky fingers through her hair. "Luke! Damn it, Luke! That is who I am supposed to be with. *Not* you!" She turns and bolts away from me, and I let her.

CHAPTER EIGHTEEN

I GO TO HER HOUSE. WE HAVE TO TALK ABOUT THIS. HER mother lets me sit in the living room until Holly decides she is ready. After a little more than an hour, I see her walking down the stairs. I stand up and walk to the door without saying a single word. Once we are both on the front steps, I close the door behind us. I don't know what comes over me, but I'm not stopping whatever it is. I pull Holly close to me and lift her chin. I slowly place my lips against hers and kiss her. I'm shocked when she leans in for more. I search her eyes for regret, but when I don't see any, I place my hand on the back of her head and pull her in for another kiss. When we finally break apart, we are both breathless. I place my forehead against hers and hold her hand. Why do I feel like an ass?

"I'm so sorry," I breathe.

She backs away from me and smiles. "Why are you apologizing?"

"I shouldn't have kissed you like that. It's just that…I have waited so long to kiss you…. I lost self-control."

In a whisper, she says, "Don't be sorry." She looks away for a moment and then looks back at me. The look in her eyes now almost takes my breath away; her expression is soft and loving, and the same one I have longed to see there for so many years. "I should be the one apologizing. I guess I've been trying to push any feelings I've had for you aside. Cohen, obviously my heart believes we are in love; it just may take my mind a little longer to catch up. I—"

I cut her off. "You have nothing to explain. I will give you all the time you need."

She smiles and her cheeks flush a beautiful soft pink. "Cohen?"

"Yeah?"

"Kiss me." I almost moan at her words. They sound so perfect. She doesn't have to tell me twice. I back her against the front door and knot my fingers into her hair. When our lips meet, I can barely control myself.

I pull away from her, and before I can even think the words, they spill from my mouth. "Holly, I love you so damn much." I kiss her slowly, pouring every emotion I've ever felt for her into this kiss. I smile against her lips as we part for air, my heart thrumming contentedly in my chest.

"What now?" she breathes.

"Now, I can kiss you and tell you I love you anytime I want."

She frowns. "But what if I don't say it back?"

"It will hurt like hell, but I won't force you to say something you're not ready to say."

She lays her head against my chest and sighs in relief. "Thank you."

PART THREE
RUMOR HAS IT

CHAPTER NINETEEN

THE PRESENT: RUMOR HAS IT...

THAT KISS. MY MIND DRIFTS BACK TO THAT MOMENT IN time and space when Holly asked me to kiss her and everything was *perfect*. It's where my memory wanders now, this one amazing thing that reminds me that I'm glad to be alive. My broken heart and the devastating emptiness left behind after losing her feels like dying.

The agonizing pain of her loss cuts so damn deep that sometimes I wish I was. The moment she looked at Luke and chose him over me and I *let* her go.... Even remembering it now feels like dying a thousand deaths, ripping my heart in two all over again. A year later, I'm doing better. Sort of. My feelings for her are still too real, but I feel like I can finally breathe again.

I look out at the waves and smile as I reminisce over all the good times we shared here. I remember when we created the paths from our houses to here. I relive every night coming here and gazing at the stars, talking about life. The time has come to say goodbye, though. I have to let Paradise go. It's the only way to set her free completely.

I'm about to turn around to leave Paradise behind forever, when I see something glinting in the light in the distance. I shade my eyes from the sun with my hand, trying to detect what it is. I walk toward it and bend down to pick it up. A tear slides down my cheek as I retrieve it and twirl it around with my fingers. Holly's Fae ring. I look inside and see *Tuff* etched carefully in the silver. I smile and place it safely in my pocket.

As I walk around the corner and my house comes into view, I stop. It can't be?! My eyes dart curiously between Jenna and the four-year-old boy standing next to her. Taking a deep breath, I swallow hard and walk closer to them.

"Cohen…" She has tears in her eyes, and I'm not sure if I should be angry with her or not.

I look down at the little boy who's peering up at me with eyes that mirror mine. I look back at Jenna, tears beginning to cloud my vision. I stutter and stumble over words until I finally say something that can be understood.

"I—…Is this *my* son?"

A few tears fall from her eyes as she nods her head. She squats down so she is eye level with my son, and does her best to smile. "Isaac, this is your father."

His little eyes meet mine again, and he smiles. He doesn't say anything, latching on to Jenna as he continues to smile up at me.

Jenna looks sheepishly at me. "I'm sorry. It may take him some time to get used to you."

I wipe tears from my eyes and fold my arms across my chest. "Where have you been?!"

She shakes her head and frowns. "We shouldn't talk about this in front of him."

I feel my hands shaking and don't even try to hide my anger. "He deserves to know just as much as I do!" I look at Isaac. At *my* son. I can see the beginnings of fear starting to creep across his face, so I take a deep breath and try to calm down.

Jenna is crying and shaking her head. "Please, Cohen…"

I walk past them and peek my head inside the house. "Mom!" I hear her walking down the hall toward me, and when she sees the gravity of my expression, she picks up her pace.

"What is it?!" she asks, looking past me to Jenna and Isaac. "Who are they?"

"I'll explain in a minute. Could you please take Isaac inside for second?"

She nods her head and joins us outside. Jenna takes Isaac's little hand and places it into my mom's waiting palm. Isaac starts to walk with her, but keeps looking back over his shoulder at Jenna.

Jenna forces a smile on her face. "It's okay, baby. You can go with her." Jenna and I both watch as they disappear into the house.

I close the door behind them and turn to face her. "Explain."

She leans against the house and begins to cry again. "I'm so sorry! I freaked, Cohen. I didn't want my parents to hate me. I didn't want to burden you with the responsibility of a child! I didn't want you to get in trouble for getting me pregnant!"

"Do you have any idea how long I've looked for the two of you?!"

"I'm sorry!" she screams in anguish.

"Sorry isn't good enough!" I yell back.

She takes a few deep, calming breaths and composes herself. "Look, I only came to bring him to you and leave again. I'm not staying."

"You're *what*?!"

"I'm so sorry, Cohen. But I can't keep your son from you any longer. He doesn't deserve to be with me, anyway. I've gotten myself into a lot of trouble, and he doesn't need to be a part of it." She starts to walk away, but I grab her arm as fear settles into every pore in my body.

"What kind of trouble! Maybe I can help?"

She laughs acidly and forcefully pries my hand from her arm. "Take care of Isaac. That's the only way you can help me now. I need to go, Cohen. Please, just promise me you'll take care of him."

I feel tears filling my eyes once again. "I don't know anything about how to be a dad! Please, just stay. I can help you get out of whatever kind of trouble you're in."

"Bye, Cohen." Jenna begins to sob hysterically and then is gone, using her teleporting abilities to disappear to who-the-hell-knows where.

I sink to my knees and run my hands through my hair, the tears spilling over. I look at my front door and my heart rate increases. My *son* is in there. All he's ever known is Jenna. And now she's gone. I watch as the door opens and my mom appears, Isaac in her arms. I quickly stand up, wiping my eyes on my shirt.

"Cohen, what's going on?" my mom asks, handing Isaac to me. As Isaac is placed in my arms, I feel like I can't breathe. I bury my head on Isaac's tiny shoulder and cry. I can't believe I am holding my son. After all these years...

I remind myself I need to be strong for him and look determinedly at my mom. "This is my son." I say, my voice cracking a bit.

"Y-your son?" she asks. Her eyes are wide with shock.

"Mom, I'm sorry I kept it from you. I was going to tell you, but when Jenna ran off, I didn't see the point." I look at Isaac, who looks scared as hell. I hug him tighter and whisper soothingly, "It's going to be okay."

My mom wipes tears from her eyes and smiles. "Where did Jenna go?" I shake my head, not saying a word. I don't want to upset Isaac more than I probably already have.

"We should probably go in and tell dad," I say, setting Isaac down. He takes me by surprise when he grabs my hand and looks up at me in confusion.

"But I thought *you* were my dad?" he says. I almost start to cry again when I hear his sweet, small voice.

I smile and kneel down so I'm eye level with him. "No, I meant *my* dad, who is also your grandfather."

He scrunches his eyebrows. "Oh. Where is my mommy?"

I give my mom a meaningful look, and she retreats back into the house. I sigh, knowing that I just need to be honest with Isaac. I refuse to lie to him.

"Son, your mom had to leave. But you're going to stay with me. Is that okay?"

I watch as his little eyes get teary, but he bravely wipes them away on his shirt. He nods his little head and reaches his arms up to me. I take that as an invitation to pick him up.

We walk toward the door, and before we go in, he says in awe, "You're really tall. Will I be as tall as you?"

I laugh. "Probably, little buddy."

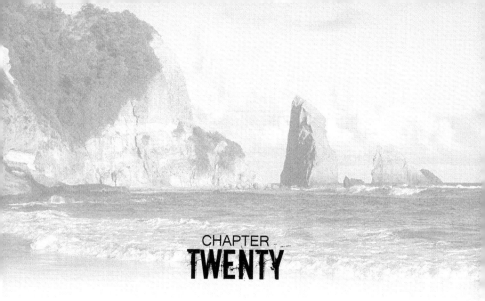

CHAPTER TWENTY

I'M A FATHER. THE REALITY HITS ME SO HARD SOMETIMES I can't breathe. I button the last button on my shirt just as Isaac walks sleepily into my room, clutching his teddy bear.

I smile and bend down to meet his eyes. Ruffling his hair I say, "Hey, you're awake early."

"I had a bad dream, Daddy."

Daddy. Hearing that word is still so surreal even though it's been a few months since his mother abandoned him and brought him to me. I pick him up as I stand and set him on the bed then sit next to him.

"Do you want to talk about it?"

He moves his teddy bear to his lap and rests his chin on its head. "No."

"Cohen!" Mom says in an outraged tone as she rushes into my room.

"Yes?" I ask in aggravation. I can't wait to move into my own place with Isaac.

"Can I have a word?"

I look at Isaac. His little nose is scrunched as he looks at mom. "What's wrong with Grams, Daddy?"

I give him a reassuring smile even though I have no clue what the hell is wrong with my mother. "Try to fall back asleep in my bed. I'll come back to check on you in a minute."

I tuck him in and walk out, closing the door behind me. I follow mom into the hall. "What's wrong with you?! You're scaring Isaac!"

"I just received word about Holly. It's not good, Cohen."

"What?!"

"She's had a child."

"Ummm…Isn't that what married people do?" To be honest, I'm crushed. It was one more thing to keep her tied to someone other than me. I know I'll never get her back. I've given up the thought of her and I the last day I visited Paradise. But I'd be lying if I didn't think about stealing her back somehow from time to time.

"Think, son! Holly is half Versipellis and half Fae."

I thought about it, but nothing made me as concerned as I felt I should be by the way mom is acting. "And?"

"And that child will be a Hybrid! It's bad enough that Holly is, but she's not pure because too much human blood runs through her veins!"

I lean against the wall as the reality of what this means sinks in. I hit the back of my head on the wall and groan.

"You stay out of it! This is her bed and now she can lie in it!" Mom states rigidly.

She knows me too well. She knows I'd go to Terre and try to help her. "But her child could be in danger! If the Regime find out or the Versipellis in Terre, who knows what they will do!" I feel my magic begin to sizzle. I do my best to concentrate on suppressing it.

The Regime was our new government. Gaia was a reign-free world until Holly didn't choose her life here. She chose a life she was never meant to have. Her becoming a Versipellis was an accident. But a majority of Gaia were worried that Luke would try to destroy our world if Holly ever mentioned loving me or trying to get back here. They said it was best to be prepared, and to make a long story short, Gaia voted and now we have the Regime.

"The Regime knows. Being that we still consider our world a world of peace, the Regime has decided to leave it alone for now. The child hasn't shown any signs of being a Hybrid but if she does, the moment it's confirmed, she will be hunted by Gaia and her own world. Hybrids are forbidden. Luke and Holly have kept her hidden from Terre and think they've hidden her from Gaia, but that isn't so."

What a mess. "Luke should know that Hybrids are forbidden! Why would he get her pregnant if there was a chance their child could be?!"

"I've never trusted King Luke, Cohen. I think he did it on purpose. Hybrids are too powerful. There were two before, a long time ago, and they were both put to death as soon as they showed their strength. They're the perfect storm. They are unstable and more powerful than a hundred Fae combined. They pose a threat to all. What if Luke planned this? What if this is all a scheme for him to be stronger than Gaia?"

"But Luke isn't like that. He killed his own parents to free Terre of their rule. As badly as I don't want to like him, he's a good guy. He came to our world to die for the wrong doings of his people."

"I think it was a pre-conceived plan."

"Mom, you've lost your mind! Luke loves Holly." Here was a possibly-legit reason to hate Luke, but for some reason I can't buy into it—as badly as I want to.

"No, he loves power. I'm not saying he doesn't love Holly, but he loves power more. He always has. I've watched his habits over the years while his parents were in rule. And I'm still convinced he's the one who killed his brother Paul, not that kid who starts with an A."

"Arlo," I mumble as I rub my temples. Mom was always up to date on the latest Terre news. This, however, was old news but she often brings it up when she gets on a rampage about Terre and the questionable rule of the Denton's.

"That whole royal family was twisted! And I just know Luke is the worst of them all!"

I place my hands in my pockets and stare down at my bare feet. I shake my head before meeting mom's eyes again. "I think you've got it all wrong, Mom."

"Maybe I do, but I want to hear you say you'll promise to stay out of it. That girl brought this trouble upon herself."

I don't answer.

"Cohen, Isaac needs you! You have a son to raise now. You can't busy yourself with something that has nothing to do with you!"

I sigh heavily when tears start to fill her eyes. "Okay. I'll *try* to stay out of it. This is the girl I love we're talking about. If for a second she or someone she loves is in danger, I can't promise I won't step in to try to help."

Mom knows there is no point in arguing. She walks off without another word. I may have let Holly go, but I'd never stop loving her. And if she ever needs me, I'll be there for her.

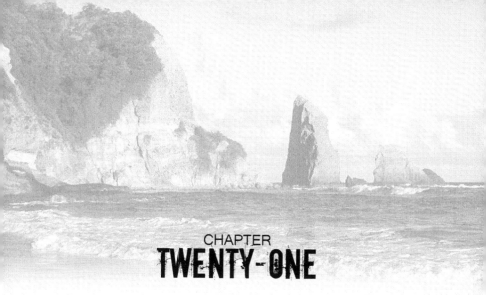

CHAPTER TWENTY-ONE

I HAVEN'T BEEN TO HOLLY'S HOUSE SINCE THE DAY I LET her go. Harim comes to check on me from time to time and to hang out with Isaac. Isaac is Uncle Harim's biggest fan.

But today. . .today I'm at her house waiting to talk to Harim about my mother's suspicions of Luke. I've given it a few months before deciding to mention it to Harim. I thought it'd blow over, but I haven't been able to get it off my mind and the Regime are anticipating the worst.

I could barely stand on the front porch while waiting to be let in. And after being let in, I feel like the walls are closing in on me. I can't stand the way everything reminds me of her. The way her house smells, the uncanny resemblance of her and her mother, and Stella, who still glares evilly at me like she always has. I wish she'd at least smile or something to make things feel somewhat different.

Not to mention the pictures. . . the damn pictures on the wall that make it all too real that Holly was once in our lives.

While I wait for Harim to get home, I make my way up the stairs. I keep waiting for Holly to come running down them to race me to Paradise. I sigh grievously.

I notice the door to her room slightly cracked open. I stop on the stairs and swallow hard. I shouldn't. . . should I? Maybe I'd find closure, or maybe going in would tear open wounds that weren't healed yet? Hell, they'd never heal.

I walk all the way up to her door and nudge it open with my foot. I lean against the door as I glance inside. Everything is the way she left it. I want to, need to, walk away. But I can't. I walk inside and jump when I hear Harim's voice from behind me.

"I was just—"

"You don't have to explain. I come in here often," he says cutting me off. "Sometimes I come in here and pretend like she's just out hanging out with you, and I'm waiting for her to come back home."

"She's never coming back."

His mouth forms a hard line. "No, she's not. She chose her path."

I back out of her room and shut the door. I turn to look at Harim. "We need to talk."

"About? Is everything okay? Is it Isaac?"

I shake my head. "No, he's fine. But I'm not sure if everything is okay."

We go to his room to talk, and there I explain everything my mom said, just leaving out the part that she possibly had a Hybrid child. I wait for him to respond. His facial expressions are always so hard to read.

"So, do you think my mom's nuts or do you think this is worth looking into?" I ask anxiously.

He looks up from the floor and at me. "You know how I feel about Terre and the Versipellis. They damn near killed my sister and took her away from her real family. I don't trust anyone from that world. But I think we all want to assume the worst so we have a reason to get Holly back. I think we need to be careful with our assumptions. The last thing we need is a war."

I nod but know I need to tell him about the child. "Well, there's more."

He raises a brow, waiting for me to explain.

"Holly and Luke had a daughter. The rumor is she is a true Hybrid. Half Fae, half Versipellis."

Harim's jaw clenches and his fists do the same. "Luke, especially being the king, would know the risks!"

"Exactly why I think my mom may be right about him." I rest my head in my hands and close my eyes. My head was pounding.

I was struggling to keep my abilities from spinning out of control. The thought of Holly and her daughter being in possible danger was too much.

"What do you suggest we do?"

I look at him. "I think the better question is what do we do if we find out my mom is right?"

"You already know the answer to that."

War. Without a doubt there'd be war, and it'd be merciless. The tension between Gaia and Terre has become increasingly worse. We've done considerably well with keeping a full out war from happening. But this would be unforgiveable. Luke better hope like hell he isn't guilty.

"Do we wait for the Regime to act or do we do our own research?"

"You have a son, Cohen. I think we should be careful with this one. We can look into it, but we need to be extremely cautious."

I nod. "I know. So, when do we start?"

"Who is watching Isaac?"

"My mom, and she said she'd watch him as long as I needed her to."

Harim stood. "Then we start now."

READ A SPECIAL PREVIEW OF
HOLLY NATHER BOOK THREE

DAUGHTER
OF A MONARCH

SARA DANIELL

THE STUNNING CONCLUSION
ARRIVES 2015

CHAPTER ONE

THESE DAMN FOUR WALLS. I'M SO SICK OF THEIR HINT OF yellow, almost mimicking the soft glow of the early rising sun. I have to get out of this room. I tuck my journal beneath my mattress.

I tiptoe through the hall and peek into my parent's room to make sure they're asleep. Once confirmed, I hurry back to my room and try to remember the spell my dad used to close the realm passage between here and Gaia. I tap my thigh as I think. Remembering, I quickly use my gift of breaking codes to release the spell.

I smile inwardly as I feel the change in temperature and know I've successfully brought myself from Terre to Gaia. I pull the ponytail holder from my wrist and quickly tie my hair in a loose bun. I throw my shoes off and bury my feet in the warm sand. *God, I missed you Gaia.*

They'd have to be crazy to think I wouldn't figure out how to return, even though they locked down travel between the worlds—*again*. I walk toward the water, and suddenly feel like I'm being watched. *Surely, I haven't been caught already?!* I turn around and see someone walking in the distance. I dart behind a tree and try to breathe as quietly and evenly as possible.

I watch as a male figure emerges from the tree line and approaches the water. He has dark hair, and I catch a quick glimpse of his green eyes. He must be one of the Fae my mother has told me about. I try to teleport myself back to Terre, but for some inconvenient as hell reason, it's not working.

I start to panic as he nears my location. I look around for another place to hide, but there isn't anywhere else to go.

Shit.

He looks around, and I know he can probably hear my ragged breathing. I've been told time after time not to come in contact with anyone outside of the castle in Terre. My parents treat outsiders like they're the plague. And because of their fear of others, I'm a social klutz.

I'm so nervous that I'm panting like I've run a marathon. I do my best to stay hidden behind the tree, but he is getting closer, and I'm shaking like a dog shitting razor blades. I tuck my hair behind my ears and put my back against the tree.

He leans his back against the tree I'm hiding behind, and I instinctively hold my breath. I start to feel lightheaded, and in my desperation for fresh air it rushes from my lungs uncontrollably, completely giving me away. He bolts away from the tree, whirling around to look directly at me.

Damn. "Hi."

"Who are you?!" he asks, studying my face and stepping closer. His eyes immediately find mine.

I step back. "Ummm, it's probably not a good idea for me to tell you that." My parents told me that the people of Gaia don't like Versipellis, especially when they're *in* Gaia. The level of prejudice between the worlds is ridiculous.

He looks confused. He shoves his hands in his pockets and mutters sullenly, "I didn't think anyone else knew about this place," he said looking at the water then back me.

"Me either," I mumble.

He smiles as he gets a better look at me. He stretches out his hand. "I'm Isaac."

I look at his hand but don't take it. "And I'm lost."

He laughs. "I'll help you find your way home if you tell me your name."

"Again. Bad idea to tell you anything about me. But you might have a hard time helping me find my way home. Don't worry. My parents will be here any minute looking for me. You might want to leave now, though, or they will probably kill us both." I sit down in the sand and rest my chin on my hand.

"What part of Gaia are you from?" he asks, sitting down next to me.

I stare at him uneasily. It makes me uncomfortable how comfortably he is interacting with me. My palms are sweaty, and I feel like I might break out in hives.

"*Aislin!*" Well, there's my mother.

I stand up and wipe sand from my legs. "Hello, Mother." She has her hands on her hips, and by the look on her face, I'm dead.

"Do you realize what we're risking by coming here?!" She is stomping toward me, and I have the sudden urge to run, but decide I better stay put if I value my life at all.

I look away from her eyes. "I'm sorry, I—"

"*Sorry?* Aislin, we have told you *repeatedly* how dangerous it is to come here! I should—" Her tirade cuts off abruptly as I watch her alarmed eyes glance over at Isaac. She studies him intently for a brief moment; then her expression instantly goes soft.

"Mom?" I'm worried about her sudden mood swing…she's never this quiet when I'm in trouble. For some reason seeing Isaac shut her up, and although it's weird, I can't peel my eyes from the scene unfolding before me.

Isaac looks scared. My mom is closing the distance between them. *Slowly.* And he is terrified. My mom on a rampage would scare even the most fearless of tyrants. I shrug my shoulders when Isaac looks to me for an explanation of her creepiness and watch as my mother continues to stare solemnly at him.

"What is your name?" she asks in a whisper, only inches from his face. Her fingers almost touch his face, but she refrains from doing so, putting her trembling hand back down by her side.

He stutters a bit before answering. "Umm, Isaac." He takes a cautious step back, adding some precious inches to his unoccupied personal space.

"Who is your father?" she pries further, her eyes searching his face intently.

"Cohen Aberdeen." I watch as my mom blanches at the sound of a man's voice coming from a patch of tall grass behind her.

My mother turns her head slowly and claps her hand to her mouth as she gasps at the sight of this man. When he walks out into the open and his gaze lands on her, his eyes widen in shock and awe.

"No way..." he chokes out. Isaac and I exchange worried looks and then turn to watch the events transpiring between them.

My mom looks down at her feet and shakes her head. Looking up at me, she says in a steady, forced-calm tone, "Aislin, we have to go."

I rush to my mom's side at the sound of fear in her voice. "Mom, what is it?!"

"*Now!*" she screams. She turns to walk away but is stopped by the man's hand on her shoulder.

"Holly?" he asks, pleading.

She takes a deep breath and turns to face him. "Cohen, you know I'm not supposed to be here."

"Wait, you know him?!" I gulp, pointing to the newcomer.

I watch a single tear slide down his cheek. "Why are you here?"

She hangs her head and sighs softly. My mother grabs my hand, and I watch as a solitary tear slides down her cheek before teleporting us back to Terre.

ACKNOWLEDGEMENTS

Mandi Cranson, Lauren Case, Kerri Bennett and Lacey Hackett for helping the story become something it wouldn't have without their help. All of you ladies rock!

ABOUT THE AUTHOR

Sara Daniell is a wife and mother who spends her days teaching children and her nights loving her family, and finding time to immerse herself into her two creative passions. In her free time she not only writes unique and amazing stories, she also takes breathtaking pictures that captures her creative nature in color just like her writings capture her creative nature in print. She is an amazing woman who loves life and people.

Made in the USA
Charleston, SC
27 December 2014